You Never Can Tell

By George Bernard Shaw

1897

This book has been published by:

Contact: sales@nuvisionpublications.com

URL: http://www.nuvisionpublications.com

Publishing Date: 2008

ISBN# 1-59547-672-5

Please see our website for several books created for
education, research and entertainment.

Specializing in rare, out-of-print books still in demand.

NuVision Publications, LLC is dedicated to bringing new life to rare, historic, and formerly out-of-print books. Most re-print publishers simply photocopy, or scan and print the pages from the original book, which can make the book hard to read as most re-print books are 100+ years old. It is our policy to take the time to convert the original faded, sometimes blotched text into crisp, clear digital text. All of our printed books have been completely reformatted to be easy to read and enjoy.

Please note that we do not correct out-of-date facts or grammar-type errors that were in the original book. We do our best to retain the original composition of the text, the way the author intended it.

NuVision Publications, LLC
Sioux Falls, SD USA

Table of Contents

Act I

In a dentist's operating room on a fine August morning in 1896. Not the usual tiny London den, but the best sitting room of a furnished lodging in a terrace on the sea front at a fashionable watering place. The operating chair, with a gas pump and cylinder beside it, is half way between the centre of the room and one of the corners. If you look into the room through the window which lights it, you will see the fireplace in the middle of the wall opposite you, with the door beside it to your left; an M.R.C.S. diploma in a frame hung on the chimneypiece; an easy chair covered in black leather on the hearth; a neat stool and bench, with vice, tools, and a mortar and pestle in the corner to the right. Near this bench stands a slender machine like a whip provided with a stand, a pedal, and an exaggerated winch. Recognising this as a dental drill, you shudder and look away to your left, where you can see another window, underneath which stands a writing table, with a blotter and a diary on it, and a chair. Next the writing table, towards the door, is a leather covered sofa. The opposite wall, close on your right, is occupied mostly by a bookcase. The operating chair is under your nose, facing you, with the cabinet of instruments handy to it on your left. You observe that the professional furniture and apparatus are new, and that the wall paper, designed, with the taste of an undertaker, in festoons and urns, the carpet with its symmetrical plans of rich, cabbagy nosegays, the glass gasalier with lustres; the ornamental gilt rimmed blue candlesticks on the ends of the mantelshelf, also glass- draped with lustres, and the ormolu clock under a glass-cover in the middle between them, its uselessness emphasized by a cheap American clock disrespectfully placed beside it and now indicating 12 o'clock noon, all combine with the black marble which gives the fireplace the air of a miniature family vault, to suggest early Victorian commercial respectability, belief in money, Bible fetishism, fear of hell always at war with fear of poverty, instinctive horror of the passionate character of art, love and Roman Catholic religion, and all the first fruits of plutocracy in the early generations of the industrial revolution.

There is no shadow of this on the two persons who are occupying the room just now. One of them, a very pretty woman in miniature, her tiny figure dressed with the daintiest gaiety, is of a later generation, being hardly eighteen yet. This darling little creature clearly does not belong to the room, or even to the country; for her complexion, though very delicate, has been burnt biscuit color by some warmer sun than England's; and yet there is, for a very subtle observer, a link between them. For she has a glass of water in her hand, and a rapidly clearing cloud of Spartan obstinacy on her tiny firm set mouth and quaintly squared eyebrows. If the least line of conscience could be traced between those eyebrows, an Evangelical might cherish some faint hope of finding her a sheep in wolf's clothing - for her frock is recklessly pretty - but as the cloud vanishes it leaves her frontal sinus as smoothly free from conviction of sin as a kitten's.

The dentist, contemplating her with the self-satisfaction of a successful operator, is a young man of thirty or thereabouts. He does not give the impression of being much of a workman: his professional manner evidently strikes him as being a joke, and is underlain by a thoughtless pleasantry which betrays the young gentleman still unsettled and in search of amusing adventures, behind the newly set-up dentist in search of patients. He is not without gravity of demeanor; but the strained nostrils stamp it as the gravity of the humorist. His eyes are clear, alert, of sceptically moderate size, and yet a little rash; his forehead is an excellent one, with plenty of room behind it; his nose and chin cavalierly handsome. On the whole, an attractive, noticeable beginner, of whose prospects a man of business might form a tolerably favorable estimate.

THE YOUNG LADY (handing him the glass). Thank you. (In spite of the biscuit complexion she has not the slightest foreign accent.)

THE DENTIST (putting it down on the ledge of his cabinet of instruments). That was my first tooth.

THE YOUNG LADY (aghast). Your first! Do you mean to say that you began practising on me?

THE DENTIST. Every dentist has to begin on somebody.

THE YOUNG LADY. Yes: somebody in a hospital, not people who pay.

THE DENTIST (laughing). Oh, the hospital doesn't count. I only meant my first tooth in private practice. Why didn't you let me give you gas?

THE YOUNG LADY. Because you said it would be five shillings extra.

THE DENTIST (shocked). Oh, don't say that. It makes me feel as if I had hurt you for the sake of five shillings.

THE YOUNG LADY (with cool insolence). Well, so you have! (She gets up.) Why shouldn't you? it's your business to hurt people. (It amuses him to be treated in this fashion: he chuckles secretly as he

8

proceeds to clean and replace his instruments. She shakes her dress into order; looks inquisitively about her; and goes to the window.) You have a good view of the sea from these rooms! Are they expensive?

THE DENTIST. Yes.

THE YOUNG LADY. You don't own the whole house, do you?

THE DENTIST. No.

THE YOUNG LADY (taking the chair which stands at the writing-table and looking critically at it as she spins it round on one leg.) Your furniture isn't quite the latest thing, is it? *goes to chair*

THE DENTIST. It's my landlord's.

THE YOUNG LADY. Does he own that nice comfortable Bath chair? (pointing to the operating chair.)

THE DENTIST. No: I have that on the hire-purchase system.

THE YOUNG LADY (disparagingly). I thought so. (Looking about her again in search of further conclusions.) I suppose you haven't been here long?

THE DENTIST. Six weeks. Is there anything else you would like to know? → *Sharp / Sarcastic*

THE YOUNG LADY (the hint quite lost on her). Any family?

THE DENTIST. I am not married.

THE YOUNG LADY. Of course not: anybody can see that. I meant sisters and mother and that sort of thing.

THE DENTIST. Not on the premises.

THE YOUNG LADY. Hm! If you've been here six weeks, and mine was your first tooth, the practice can't be very large, can it?

THE DENTIST. Not as yet. (He ~~shuts the cabinet, having tidied~~ up ~~everything.~~) *Cleans tools .*

THE YOUNG LADY. Well, good luck! (She takes our her purse.) Five shillings, you said it would be?

THE DENTIST. Five shillings.

THE YOUNG LADY (producing a crown piece). Do you charge five shillings for everything?

9

THE DENTIST. Yes.

THE YOUNG LADY. Why?

THE DENTIST. It's my system. I'm what's called a five shilling dentist.

THE YOUNG LADY. How nice! Well, here! (holding up the crown piece) a nice new five shilling piece! your first fee! Make a hole in it with the thing you drill people's teeth with and wear it on your watch-chain.

THE DENTIST. Thank you.

THE PARLOR MAID (appearing at the door). The young lady's brother, sir.

A handsome man in miniature, obviously the young lady's twin, comes in eagerly. He wears a suit of terra-cotta cashmere, the elegantly cut frock coat lined in brown silk, and carries in his hand a brown tall hat and tan gloves to match. He has his sister's delicate biscuit complexion, and is built on the same small scale; but he is elastic and strong in muscle, decisive in movement, unexpectedly deeptoned and trenchant in speech, and with perfect manners and a finished personal style which might be envied by a man twice his age. Suavity and self- possession are points of honor with him; and though this, rightly considered, is only the modern mode of boyish self-consciousness, its effect is none the less staggering to his elders, and would be insufferable in a less prepossessing youth. He is promptitude itself, and has a question ready the moment he enters.

THE YOUNG GENTLEMAN. Am I on time?

THE YOUNG LADY. No: it's all over.

THE YOUNG GENTLEMAN. Did you howl?

THE YOUNG LADY. Oh, something awful. Mr. Valentine: this is my brother Phil. Phil: this is Mr. Valentine, our new dentist. (Valentine and Phil bow to one another. She proceeds, all in one breath.) He's only been here six weeks; and he's a bachelor. The house isn't his; and the furniture is the landlord's; but the professional plant is hired. He got my tooth out beautifully at the first go; and he and I are great friends.

PHILIP. Been asking a lot of questions?

THE YOUNG LADY (as if incapable of doing such a thing). Oh, no.

PHILIP. Glad to hear it. (To Valentine.) So good of you not to mind us, Mr. Valentine. The fact is, we've never been in England before; and our mother tells us that the people here simply won't stand us. Come and lunch with us. (Valentine, bewildered by the leaps and bounds with which their acquaintanceship is proceeding, gasps; but he has no opportunity of speaking, as the conversation of the twins is swift and continuous.)

THE YOUNG LADY. Oh, do, Mr. Valentine.

PHILIP. At the Marine Hotel - half past one.

THE YOUNG LADY. We shall be able to tell mamma that a respectable Englishman has promised to lunch with us.

PHILIP. Say no more, Mr. Valentine: you'll come.

VALENTINE. Say no more! I haven't said anything. May I ask whom I have the pleasure of entertaining? It's really quite impossible for me to lunch at the Marine Hotel with two perfect strangers.

THE YOUNG LADY (flippantly). Ooooh! what bosh! One patient in six weeks! What difference does it make to you?

PHILIP (maturely). No, Dolly: my knowledge of human nature confirms Mr. Valentine's judgment. He is right. Let me introduce Miss Dorothy Clandon, commonly called Dolly. (Valentine bows to Dolly. She nods to him.) I'm Philip Clandon. We're from Madeira, but perfectly respectable, so far.) high + mighty.

VALENTINE. Clandon! Are you related to ---

DOLLY (unexpectedly crying out in despair). Yes, we are.

VALENTINE (astonished). I beg your pardon?

DOLLY. Oh, we are, we are. It's all over, Phil: they know all about us in England. (To Valentine.) Oh, you can't think how maddening it is to be related to a celebrated person, and never be valued anywhere for our own sakes.

VALENTINE. But excuse me: the gentleman I was thinking of is not celebrated.

DOLLY (staring at him). Gentleman! (Phil is also puzzled.)

VALENTINE. Yes. I was going to ask whether you were by any chance a daughter of Mr. Densmore Clandon of Newbury Hall.

DOLLY (vacantly). No.

PHILIP. Well come, Dolly: how do you know you're not?

DOLLY (cheered). Oh, I forgot. Of course. Perhaps I am.

VALENTINE. Don't you know?

PHILIP. Not in the least.

DOLLY. It's a wise child ---

PHILIP (cutting her short). Sh! (Valentine starts nervously; for the sound made by Philip, though but momentary, is like cutting a sheet of silk in two with a flash of lightning. It is the result of long practice in checking Dolly's indiscretions.) The fact is, Mr. Valentine, we are the children of the celebrated Mrs. Lanfrey Clandon, an authoress of great repute - in Madeira. No household is complete without her works. We came to England to get away from them. The are called the Twentieth Century Treatises. *advance on him*

DOLLY. Twentieth Century Cooking.

PHILIP. Twentieth Century Creeds.

DOLLY. Twentieth Century Clothing.

PHILIP. Twentieth Century Conduct.

DOLLY. Twentieth Century Children.

PHILIP. Twentieth Century Parents.

DOLLY. Cloth limp, half a dollar.

PHILIP. Or mounted on linen for hard family use, two dollars. No family should be without them. Read them, Mr. Valentine: they'll improve your mind. *Contact → touch Valentine*

DOLLY. But not till we've gone, please.

PHILIP. Quite so: we prefer people with unimproved minds. Our own minds are in that fresh and unspoiled condition.

VALENTINE (dubiously). Hm!

DOLLY (echoing him inquiringly). Hm? Phil: he prefers people whose minds are improved.

PHILIP. In that case we shall have to introduce him to the other member of the family: the Woman of the Twentieth Century; our sister Gloria!   *emphasis*

DOLLY (dithyrambically). Nature's masterpiece!

PHILIP. Learning's daughter!

DOLLY. Madeira's pride!

PHILIP. Beauty's paragon!

DOLLY (suddenly descending to prose). Bosh! No complexion.

VALENTINE (desperately). May I have a word?

PHILIP (politely). Excuse us. Go ahead.

DOLLY (very nicely). So sorry.   *more then*

VALENTINE (attempting to take them paternally). I really must give a hint to you young people---

DOLLY (breaking out again). Oh, come: I like that. How old are you?

PHILIP. Over thirty.

DOLLY. He's not.

PHILIP (confidently). He is.

DOLLY (emphatically). Twenty-seven.

PHILIP (imperturbably). Thirty-three.

DOLLY. Stuff!

PHILIP (to Valentine). I appeal to you, Mr. Valentine.

VALENTINE (remonstrating). Well, really---(resigning himself.) Thirty-one.

PHILIP (to Dolly). You were wrong.

DOLLY. So were you.

PHILIP (suddenly conscientious). We're forgetting our manners, Dolly.

DOLLY (remorseful). Yes, so we are.

PHILIP (apologetic). We interrupted you, Mr. Valentine.

DOLLY. You were going to improve our minds, I think.

VALENTINE. The fact is, your---

PHILIP (anticipating him). Our appearance?

DOLLY. Our manners?

VALENTINE (ad misericordiam). Oh, do let me speak.

DOLLY. The old story. We talk too much.

PHILIP. We do. Shut up, both. (He seats himself on the arm of the opposing chair.)

DOLLY. Mum! (She sits down in the writing-table chair, and closes her lips tight with the tips of her fingers.) *offer them a seat*

VALENTINE. Thank you. (He brings the stool from the bench in the corner; places it between them; and sits down with a judicial air. They attend to him with extreme gravity. He addresses himself first to Dolly.) Now may I ask, to begin with, have you ever been in an English seaside resort before? (She shakes her head slowly and solemnly. He turns to Phil, who shakes his head quickly and expressively.) I thought so. Well, Mr. Clandon, our acquaintance has been short; but it has been voluble; and I have gathered enough to convince me that you are neither of you capable of conceiving what life in an English seaside resort is. Believe me, it's not a question of manners and appearance. In those respects we enjoy a freedom unknown in Madeira. (Dolly shakes her head vehemently.) Oh, yes, I assure you. Lord de Cresci's sister bicycles in knickerbockers; and the rector's wife advocates dress reform and wears hygienic boots. (Dolly furtively looks at her own shoe: Valentine catches her in the act, and deftly adds) No, that's not the sort of boot I mean. (Dolly's shoe vanishes.) We don't bother much about dress and manners in England, because, as a nation we don't dress well and we've no manners. But - and now will you excuse my frankness? (They nod.) Thank you. Well, in a seaside resort there's one thing you must have before anybody can afford to be seen going about with you; and that's a father, alive or dead. (He looks at them alternately, with emphasis. They meet his gaze like martyrs.) Am I to infer that you have omitted that indispensable part of your social equipment? (They confirm him by melancholy nods.) Them I'm sorry to say that if you are going to stay here for any length of time, it will be impossible for me to accept your kind invitation to lunch. (He rises with an air of finality, and replaces the stool by the bench.)

14

cheesed off

PHILIP (rising with grave politeness). Come, Dolly. (He gives her his arm.)

DOLLY. Good morning. (They go together to the door with perfect dignity.)

VALENTINE (overwhelmed with remorse). Oh, stop, stop. (They halt and turn, arm in arm.) You make me feel a perfect beast.

DOLLY. That's your conscience: not us.

VALENTINE (energetically, throwing off all pretence of a professional manner). My conscience! My conscience has been my ruin. Listen to me. Twice before I have set up as a respectable medical practitioner in various parts of England. On both occasions I acted conscientiously, and told my patients the brute truth instead of what they wanted to be told. Result, ruin. Now I've set up as a dentist, a five shilling dentist; and I've done with conscience forever. This is my last chance. I spent my last sovereign on moving in; and I haven't paid a shilling of rent yet. I'm eating and drinking on credit; my landlord is as rich as a Jew and as hard as nails; and I've made five shillings in six weeks. If I swerve by a hair's breadth from the straight line of the most rigid respectability, I'm done for. Under such a circumstance, is it fair to ask me to lunch with you when you don't know your own father? *accusing*

DOLLY. After all, our grandfather is a canon of Lincoln Cathedral.

VALENTINE (like a castaway mariner who sees a sail on the horizon). What! Have you a grandfather?

DOLLY. Only one.

VALENTINE. My dear, good young friends, why on earth didn't you tell me that before? A cannon of Lincoln! That makes it all right, of course. Just excuse me while I change my coat. (He reaches the door in a bound and vanishes. Dolly and Phil stare after him, and then stare at one another. Missing their audience, they droop and become commonplace at once.)

PHILIP (throwing away Dolly's arm and coming ill-humoredly towards the operating chair). That wretched bankrupt ivory snatcher makes a compliment of allowing us to stand him a lunch - probably the first square meal he has had for months. (He gives the chair a kick, as if it were Valentine.)

DOLLY. It's too beastly. I won't stand it any longer, Phil. Here in England everybody asks whether you have a father the very first thing.

PHILIP. I won't stand it either. Mamma must tell us who he was.

15

DOLLY. Or who he is. He may be alive.

PHILIP. I hope not. No man alive shall father me.

DOLLY. He might have a lot of money, though.

PHILIP. I doubt it. My knowledge of human nature leads me to believe that if he had a lot of money he wouldn't have got rid of his affectionate family so easily. Anyhow, let's look at the bright side of things. Depend on it, he's dead. (He goes to the hearth and stands with his back to the fireplace, spreading himself. The parlor maid appears. The twins, under observation, instantly shine out again with their former brilliancy.)

THE PARLOR MAID. Two ladies for you, miss. Your mother and sister, miss, I think.

MRS. CLANDON and Gloria come in. Mrs. Clandon is between forty and fifty, with a slight tendency to soft, sedentary fat, and a fair remainder of good looks, none the worse preserved because she has evidently followed the old tribal matronly fashion of making no pretension in that direction after her marriage, and might almost be suspected of wearing a cap at home. She carries herself artificially well, as women were taught to do as a part of good manners by dancing masters and reclining boards before these were superseded by the modern artistic cult of beauty and health. Her hair, a flaxen hazel fading into white, is crimped, and parted in the middle with the ends plaited and made into a knot, from which observant people of a certain age infer that Mrs. Clandon had sufficient individuality and good taste to stand out resolutely against the now forgotten chignon in her girlhood. In short, she is distinctly old fashioned for her age in dress and manners. But she belongs to the forefront of her own period (say 1860-80) in a jealously assertive attitude of character and intellect, and in being a woman of cultivated interests rather than passionately developed personal affections. Her voice and ways are entirely kindly and humane; and she lends herself conscientiously to the occasional demonstrations of fondness by which her children mark their esteem for her; but displays of personal sentiment secretly embarrass her: passion in her is humanitarian rather than human: she feels strongly about social questions and principles, not about persons. Only, one observes that this reasonableness and intense personal privacy, which leaves her relations with Gloria and Phil much as they might be between her and the children of any other woman, breaks down in the case of Dolly. Though almost every word she addresses to her is necessarily in the nature of a remonstrance for some breach of decorum, the tenderness in her voice is unmistakable; and it is not surprising that years of such remonstrance have left Dolly hopelessly spoiled.

GLORIA, who is hardly past twenty, is a much more formidable person than her mother. She is the incarnation of haughty highmindedness, raging with the impatience of an impetuous, dominative character paralyzed by the impotence of her youth, and unwillingly disciplined by the constant danger of ridicule from her lighter-handed juniors. Unlike her mother, she is all passion; and the conflict of her passion with her obstinate pride and intense fastidiousness results in a freezing coldness of manner. In an ugly woman all this would be repulsive; but Gloria is an attractive woman. Her deep chestnut hair, olive brown skin, long eyelashes, shaded grey eyes that often flash like stars, delicately turned full lips, and compact and supple, but muscularly plump figure appeal with disdainful frankness to the senses and imagination. A very dangerous girl, one would say, if the moral passions were not also marked, and even nobly marked, in a fine brow. Her tailor-made skirt-and-jacket dress of saffron brown cloth, seems conventional when her back is turned; but it displays in front a blouse of sea-green silk which upsets its conventionality with one stroke, and sets her apart as effectually as the twins from the ordinary run of fashionable seaside humanity.

MRS. CLANDON comes a little way into the room, looking round to see who is present. Gloria, who studiously avoids encouraging the twins by betraying any interest in them, wanders to the window and looks out with her thoughts far away. The parlor maid, instead of withdrawing, shuts the door and waits at it.

MRS. CLANDON. Well, children? How is the toothache, Dolly?

DOLLY. Cured, thank Heaven. I've had it out. (She sits down on the step of the operating chair. Mrs. Clandon takes the writing-table chair.)

PHILIP (striking in gravely from the hearth). And the dentist, a first-rate professional man of the highest standing, is coming to lunch with us.

MRS. CLANDON (looking round apprehensively at the servant). Phil!

THE PARLOR MAID. Beg pardon, ma'am. I'm waiting for Mr. Valentine. I have a message for him.

DOLLY. Who from?

MRS. CLANDON (shocked). Dolly! (Dolly catches her lips with her finger tips, suppressing a little splutter of mirth.)

THE PARLOR MAID. Only the landlord, ma'am.

VALENTINE, in a blue serge suit, with a straw hat in his hand, comes back in high spirits, out of breath with the haste he has made. Gloria turns from the window and studies him with freezing attention.

PHILIP. Let me introduce you, Mr. Valentine. My mother, Mrs. Lanfrey Clandon. (Mrs. Clandon bows. Valentine bows, self-possessed and quite equal to the occasion.) My sister Gloria. (Gloria bows with cold dignity and sits down on the sofa. Valentine falls in love at first sight and is miserably confused. He fingers his hat nervously, and makes her a sneaking bow.) *Valentine gestures to sit*

MRS. CLANDON. I understand that we are to have the pleasure of seeing you at luncheon to-day, Mr. Valentine.

VALENTINE. Thank you--er--if you don't mind--I mean if you will be so kind -- (to the parlor maid testily) What is it?

THE PARLOR MAID. The landlord, sir, wishes to speak to you before you go out.

VALENTINE. Oh, tell him I have four patients here. (The Clandons look surprised, except Phil, who is imperturbable.) If he wouldn't mind waiting just two minutes, I--I'll slip down and see him for a moment. (Throwing himself confidentially on her sense of the position.) Say I'm busy, but that I want to see him.

THE PARLOR MAID (reassuringly). Yes, sir. (She goes.)

MRS. CLANDON (on the point of rising). We are detaining you, I am afraid. *gesture to sit*

VALENTINE. Not at all, not at all. Your presence here will be the greatest help to me. The fact is, I owe six week's rent; and I've had no patients until to-day. My interview with my landlord will be considerably smoothed by the apparent boom in my business.

DOLLY (vexed). Oh, how tiresome of you to let it all out! And we've just been pretending that you were a respectable professional man in a first-rate position.

MRS. CLANDON (horrified). Oh, Dolly, Dolly! My dearest, how can you be so rude? (To Valentine.) Will you excuse these barbarian children of mine, Mr. Valentine?

VALENTINE. Thank you, I'm used to them. Would it be too much to ask you to wait five minutes while I get rid of my landlord downstairs?

DOLLY. Don't be long. We're hungry.

MRS. CLANDON (again remonstrating). Dolly, dear!

VALENTINE (to Dolly). All right. (To Mrs. Clandon.) Thank you: I shan't be long. (He steals a look at Gloria as he turns to go. She is looking gravely at him. He falls into confusion.) I--er--er--yes-- thank

18

you (he succeeds at last in blundering himself out of the room; but the exhibition is a pitiful one).

PHILIP. Did you observe? (Pointing to Gloria.) Love at first sight. You can add his scalp to your collection, Gloria.

MRS. CLANDON. Sh--sh, pray, Phil. He may have heard you.

PHILIP. Not he. (Bracing himself for a scene.) And now look here, mamma. (He takes the stool from the bench; and seats himself majestically in the middle of the room, taking a leaf out of Valentine's book. Dolly, feeling that her position on the step of the operating chair is unworthy of the dignity of the occasion, rises, looking important and determined; crosses to the window; and stands with her back to the end of the writing-table, her hands behind her and on the table. Mrs. Clandon looks at them, wondering what is coming. Gloria becomes attentive. Philip straightens his back; places his knuckles symmetrically on his knees; and opens his case.) Dolly and I have been talking over things a good deal lately; and I don't think, judging from my knowledge of human nature--we don't think that you (speaking very staccato, with the words detached) quite appreciate the fact ---

DOLLY (seating herself on the end of the table with a spring). That we've grown up.

MRS. CLANDON. Indeed? In what way have I given you any reason to complain?

PHILIP. Well, there are certain matters upon which we are beginning to feel that you might take us a little more into your confidence.

MRS. CLANDON (rising, with all the placidity of her age suddenly broken up; and a curious hard excitement, dignified but dogged, ladylike but implacable--the manner of the Old Guard of the Women's Rights movement--coming upon her). Phil: take care. Remember what I have always taught you. There are two sorts of family life, Phil; and your experience of human nature only extends, so far, to one of them. (Rhetorically.) The sort you know is based on mutual respect, on recognition of the right of every member of the household to independence and privacy (her emphasis on "privacy" is intense) in their personal concerns. And because you have always enjoyed that, it seems such a matter of course to you that you don't value it. But (with biting acrimony) there is another sort of family life: a life in which husbands open their wives' letters, and call on them to account for every farthing of their expenditure and every moment of their time; in which women do the same to their children; in which no room is private and no hour sacred; in which duty, obedience, affection, home, morality and religion are detestable tyrannies, and life is a vulgar round of punishments and lies, coercion and rebellion, jealousy, suspicion, recrimination--Oh! I cannot describe it to you: fortunately for you, you

19

know nothing about it. (She sits down, panting. Gloria has listened to her with flashing eyes, sharing all her indignation.)

DOLLY (inaccessible to rhetoric). See Twentieth Century Parents, chapter on Liberty, passim.

MRS. CLANDON (touching her shoulder affectionately, soothed even by a gibe from her). My dear Dolly: if you only knew how glad I am that it is nothing but a joke to you, though it is such bitter earnest to me. (More resolutely, turning to Philip.) Phil, I never ask you questions about your private concerns. You are not going to question me, are you?

PHILIP. I think it due to ourselves to say that the question we wanted to ask is as much our business as yours.

DOLLY. Besides, it can't be good to keep a lot of questions bottled up inside you. You did it, mamma; but see how awfully it's broken out again in me.

MRS. CLANDON. I see you want to ask your question. Ask it.

short !

DOLLY AND PHILIP (beginning simultaneously). Who--- (They stop.)

PHILIP. Now look here, Dolly: am I going to conduct this business or are you?

DOLLY. You.   *pinch it.*

PHILIP. Then hold your mouth. (Dolly does so literally.) The question is a simple one. When the ivory snatcher---

MRS. CLANDON (remonstrating). Phil!

PHILIP. Dentist is an ugly word. The man of ivory and gold asked us whether we were the children of Mr. Densmore Clandon of Newbury Hall. In pursuance of the precepts in your treatise on Twentieth Century Conduct, and your repeated personal exhortations to us to curtail the number of unnecessary lies we tell, we replied truthfully the we didn't know. *Pace   -airs + graces .*

DOLLY. Neither did we.

PHILIP. Sh! The result was that the gum architect made considerable difficulties about accepting our invitation to lunch, although I doubt if he has had anything but tea and bread and butter for a fortnight past. Now my knowledge of human nature leads me to believe that we had a father, and that you probably know who he was.

MRS. CLANDON (her agitation returning). Stop, Phil. Your father is nothing to you, nor to me (vehemently). That is enough. (The twins are silenced, but not satisfied. Their faces fall. But Gloria, who has been following the altercation attentively, suddenly intervenes.)

GLORIA (advancing). Mother: we have a right to know.

MRS. CLANDON (rising and facing her). Gloria! "We!" Who is "we"?

GLORIA (steadfastly). We three. (Her tone is unmistakable: she is pitting her strength against her mother for the first time. The twins instantly go over to the enemy.)

MRS. CLANDON (wounded). In your mouth "we" used to mean you and I, Gloria.

PHILIP (rising decisively and putting away the stool). We're hurting you: let's drop it. We didn't think you'd mind. I don't want to know.

DOLLY (coming off the table). I'm sure I don't. Oh, don't look like that, mamma. (She looks angrily at Gloria.)

MRS. CLANDON (touching her eyes hastily with her handkerchief and sitting down again). Thank you, my dear. Thanks, Phil.

GLORIA (inexorably). We have a right to know, mother.

MRS. CLANDON (indignantly). Ah! You insist.

GLORIA. Do you intend that we shall never know?

DOLLY. Oh, Gloria, don't. It's barbarous.

GLORIA (with quiet scorn). What is the use of being weak? You see what has happened with this gentleman here, mother. The same thing has happened to me.

MRS. CLANDON	} (all	{ What do you mean?
DOLLY	} together).	{ Oh, tell us.
PHILIP	}	{ What happened to you?

GLORIA. Oh, nothing of any consequence. (She turns away from them and goes up to the easy chair at the fireplace, where she sits down, almost with her back to them. As they wait expectantly, she adds, over her shoulder, with studied indifference.) On board the steamer the first officer did me the honor to propose to me.

DOLLY. No, it was to me.

21

MRS. CLANDON. The first officer! Are you serious, Gloria? What did you say to him? (correcting herself) Excuse me: I have no right to ask that.

GLORIA. The answer is pretty obvious. A woman who does not know who her father was cannot accept such an offer.

MRS. CLANDON. Surely you did not want to accept it?

GLORIA (turning a little and raising her voice). No; but suppose I had wanted to!

PHILIP. Did that difficulty strike you, Dolly?

DOLLY. No, I accepted him.

GLORIA	} (all crying	{ Accepted him!
MRS. CLANDON	} out	{ Dolly!
PHILIP	} together)	{ Oh, I say!

DOLLY (naively). He did look such a fool!

MRS. CLANDON. But why did you do such a thing, Dolly?

DOLLY. For fun, I suppose. He had to measure my finger for a ring. You'd have done the same thing yourself.

MRS. CLANDON. No, Dolly, I would not. As a matter of fact the first officer did propose to me, and I told him to keep that sort of thing for women were young enough to be amused by it. He appears to have acted on my advice. (She rises and goes to the hearth.) Gloria: I am sorry you think me weak; but I cannot tell you what you want. You are all too young.

PHILIP. This is rather a startling departure from Twentieth Century principles.

DOLLY (quoting). "Answer all your children's questions, and answer them truthfully, as soon as they are old enough to ask them." See Twentieth Century Motherhood---

PHILIP. Page one---

DOLLY. Chapter one---

PHILIP. Sentence one.

22

stay seated

MRS. CLANDON. My dears: I did not say that you were too young to know. I said you were too young to be taken into my confidence. You are very bright children, all of you; but I am glad for your sakes that you are still very inexperienced and consequently very unsympathetic. There are some experiences of mine that I cannot bear to speak of except to those who have gone through what I have gone through. I hope you will never be qualified for such confidences. But I will take care that you shall learn all you want to know. Will that satisfy you?

PHILIP. Another grievance, Dolly.

DOLLY. We're not sympathetic.

GLORIA (leaning forward in her chair and looking earnestly up at her mother). Mother: I did not mean to be unsympathetic.

MRS. CLANDON (affectionately). Of course not, dear. Do you think I don't understand?

GLORIA (rising). But, mother---

MRS. CLANDON (drawing back a little). Yes?

GLORIA (obstinately). It is nonsense to tell us that our father is nothing to us.

MRS. CLANDON (provoked to sudden resolution). Do you remember your father?

GLORIA (meditatively, as if the recollection were a tender one). I am not quite sure. I think so.

MRS. CLANDON (grimly). You are not sure?

GLORIA. No.

MRS. CLANDON (with quiet force). Gloria: if I had ever struck you-- (Gloria recoils: Philip and Dolly are disagreeably shocked; all three start at her, revolted as she continues)--struck you purposely, deliberately, with the intention of hurting you, with a whip bought for the purpose! Would you remember that, do you think? (Gloria utters an exclamation of indignant repulsion.) That would have been your last recollection of your father, Gloria, if I had not taken you away from him. I have kept him out of your life: keep him now out of mine by never mentioning him to me again. (Gloria, with a shudder, covers her face with her hands, until, hearing someone at the door, she turns away and pretends to occupy herself looking at the names of the books in the bookcase. Mrs. Clandon sits down on the sofa. Valentine returns.).

round the chair + held on

23

VALENTINE. I hope I've not kept you waiting. That landlord of mine is really an extraordinary old character.

DOLLY (eagerly). Oh, tell us. How long has he given you to pay?

MRS. CLANDON (distracted by her child's bad manners). Dolly, Dolly, Dolly dear! You must not ask questions.

DOLLY (demurely). So sorry. You'll tell us, won't you, Mr. Valentine?

VALENTINE. He doesn't want his rent at all. He's broken his tooth on a Brazil nut; and he wants me to look at it and to lunch with him afterwards.

DOLLY. Then have him up and pull his tooth out at once; and we'll bring him to lunch, too. Tell the maid to fetch him along. (She runs to the bell and rings it vigorously. Then, with a sudden doubt she turns to Valentine and adds) I suppose he's respectable---really respectable.

VALENTINE. Perfectly. Not like me.

DOLLY. Honest Injun? (Mrs. Clandon gasps faintly; but her powers of remonstrance are exhausted.)

VALENTINE. Honest Injun!

DOLLY. Then off with you and bring him up.

VALENTINE (looking dubiously at Mrs. Clandon). I daresay he'd be delighted if--er---?

MRS. CLANDON (rising and looking at her watch). I shall be happy to see your friend at lunch, if you can persuade him to come; but I can't wait to see him now: I have an appointment at the hotel at a quarter to one with an old friend whom I have not seen since I left England eighteen years ago. Will you excuse me?

VALENTINE. Certainly, Mrs. Clandon.

GLORIA. Shall I come?

MRS. CLANDON. No, dear. I want to be alone. (She goes out, evidently still a good deal troubled. Valentine opens the door for her and follows her out.)

PHILIP (significantly--to Dolly). Hmhm!

DOLLY (significantly to Philip). Ahah! (The parlor maid answers the bell.)

DOLLY. Show the old gentleman up.

THE PARLOR MAID (puzzled). Madam?

DOLLY. The old gentleman with the toothache.

PHILIP. The landlord.

THE PARLOR MAID. Mr. Crampton, Sir?

PHILIP. Is his name Crampton?

DOLLY (to Philip). Sounds rheumaticky, doesn't it?

PHILIP. Chalkstones, probably.

DOLLY (over her shoulder, to the parlor maid). Show Mr. Crampstones up. (Goes R. to writing-table chair).

THE PARLOR MAID (correcting her). Mr. Crampton, miss. (She goes.)

DOLLY (repeating it to herself like a lesson). Crampton, Crampton, Crampton, Crampton, Crampton. (She sits down studiously at the writing- table.) I must get that name right, or Heaven knows what I shall call him.

GLORIA. Phil: can you believe such a horrible thing as that about our father---what mother said just now?

PHILIP. Oh, there are lots of people of that kind. Old Chalice used to thrash his wife and daughters with a cartwhip.

DOLLY (contemptuously). Yes, a Portuguese! *eck*

PHILIP. When you come to men who are brutes, there is much in common between the Portuguese and the English variety, Doll. Trust my knowledge of human nature. (He resumes his position on the hearthrug with an elderly and responsible air.)

GLORIA (with angered remorse). I don't think we shall ever play again at our old game of guessing what our father was to be like. Dolly: are you sorry for your father---the father with lots of money?

DOLLY. Oh, come! What about your father---the lonely old man with the tender aching heart? He's pretty well burst up, I think.

PHILIP. There can be no doubt that the governor is an exploded superstition. (Valentine is heard talking to somebody outside the door.) But hark: he comes.

25

GLORIA (nervously). Who?

DOLLY. Chalkstones.

PHILIP. Sh! Attention. (They put on their best manners. Philip adds in a lower voice to Gloria) If he's good enough for the lunch, I'll nod to Dolly; and if she nods to you, invite him straight away.

(Valentine comes back with his landlord. Mr. Fergus Crampton is a man of about sixty, tall, hard and stringy, with an atrociously obstinate, ill tempered, grasping mouth, and a querulously dogmatic voice. Withal he is highly nervous and sensitive, judging by his thin transparent skin marked with multitudinous lines, and his slender fingers. His consequent capacity for suffering acutely from all the dislike that his temper and obstinacy can bring upon him is proved by his wistful, wounded eyes, by a plaintive note in his voice, a painful want of confidence in his welcome, and a constant but indifferently successful effort to correct his natural incivility of manner and proneness to take offence. By his keen brows and forehead he is clearly a shrewd man; and there is no sign of straitened means or commercial diffidence about him: he is well dressed, and would be classed at a guess as a prosperous master manufacturer in a business inherited from an old family in the aristocracy of trade. His navy blue coat is not of the usual fashionable pattern. It is not exactly a pilot's coat; but it is cut that way, double breasted, and with stout buttons and broad lappels, a coat for a shipyard rather than a counting house. He has taken a fancy to Valentine, who cares nothing for his crossness of grain and treats him with a sort of disrespectful humanity, for which he is secretly grateful.)

VALENTINE. May I introduce---this is Mr. Crampton---Miss Dorothy Clandon, Mr. Philip Clandon, Miss Clandon. (Crampton stands nervously bowing. They all bow.) Sit down, Mr. Crampton.

DOLLY (pointing to the operating chair). That is the most comfortable chair, Mr. Ch--crampton.

CRAMPTON. Thank you; but won't this young lady---(indicating Gloria, who is close to the chair)?

GLORIA. Thank you, Mr. Crampton: we are just going.

VALENTINE (bustling him across to the chair with good-humored peremptoriness). Sit down, sit down. You're tired.

CRAMPTON. Well, perhaps as I am considerably the oldest person present, I--- (He finishes the sentence by sitting down a little rheumatically in the operating chair. Meanwhile, Philip, having studied him critically during his passage across the room, nods to Dolly; and Dolly nods to Gloria.)

26

GLORIA. Mr. Crampton: we understand that we are preventing Mr. Valentine from lunching with you by taking him away ourselves. My mother would be very glad, indeed, if you would come too.

CRAMPTON (gratefully, after looking at her earnestly for a moment). Thank you. I will come with pleasure.

GLORIA	} (politely	{ Thank you very much--er---
DOLLY	} murmuring).	{ So glad--er---
PHILIP	}	{ Delighted, I'm sure--er---

(The conversation drops. Gloria and Dolly look at one another; then at Valentine and Philip. Valentine and Philip, unequal to the occasion, look away from them at one another, and are instantly so disconcerted by catching one another's eye, that they look back again and catch the eyes of Gloria and Dolly. Thus, catching one another all round, they all look at nothing and are quite at a loss. Crampton looks about him, waiting for them to begin. The silence becomes unbearable.)

DOLLY (suddenly, to keep things going). How old are you, Mr. Crampton?

GLORIA (hastily). I am afraid we must be going, Mr. Valentine. It is understood, then, that we meet at half past one. (She makes for the door. Philip goes with her. Valentine retreats to the bell.)

VALENTINE. Half past one. (He rings the bell.) Many thanks. (He follows Gloria and Philip to the door, and goes out with them.)

DOLLY (who has meanwhile stolen across to Crampton). Make him give you gas. It's five shillings extra: but it's worth it.

CRAMPTON (amused). Very well. (Looking more earnestly at her.) So you want to know my age, do you? I'm fifty-seven.

DOLLY (with conviction). You look it.

CRAMPTON (grimly). I dare say I do.

DOLLY. What are you looking at me so hard for? Anything wrong? (She feels whether her hat is right.)

CRAMPTON. You're like somebody.

DOLLY. Who?

CRAMPTON. Well, you have a curious look of my mother.

DOLLY (incredulously). Your mother!!! Quite sure you don't mean your daughter?

CRAMPTON (suddenly blackening with hate). Yes: I'm quite sure I don't mean my daughter.

DOLLY (sympathetically). Tooth bad?

CRAMPTON. No, no: nothing. A twinge of memory, Miss Clandon, not of toothache.

DOLLY. Have it out. "Pluck from the memory a rooted sorrow:" with gas, five shillings extra.

pissed

CRAMPTON (vindicatively). No, not a sorrow. An injury that was done me once: that's all. I don't forget injuries; and I don't want to forget them. (His features settle into an implacable frown.)

(re-enter Philip: to look for Dolly. He comes down behind her unobserved.)

DOLLY (looking critically at Crampton's expression). I don't think we shall like you when you are brooding over your sorrows.

PHILIP (who has entered the room unobserved, and stolen behind her). My sister means well, Mr. Crampton: but she is indiscreet. Now Dolly, outside! (He takes her towards the door.)

DOLLY (in a perfectly audible undertone). He says he's only fifty-seven; and he thinks me the image of his mother; and he hates his daughter; and--- (She is interrupted by the return of Valentine.)

VALENTINE. Miss Clandon has gone on.

PHILIP. Don't forget half past one.

gesture to him ←

DOLLY. Mind you leave Mr. Crampton with enough teeth to eat with. (They go out. Valentine comes down to his cabinet, and opens it.)

CRAMPTON. That's a spoiled child, Mr. Valentine. That's one of your modern products. When I was her age, I had many a good hiding fresh in my memory to teach me manners.

VALENTINE (taking up his dental mirror and probe from the shelf in front of the cabinet). What did you think of her sister?

CRAMPTON. You liked her better, eh?

VALENTINE (rhapsodically). She struck me as being--- (He checks himself, and adds, prosaically) However, that's not business. (He places himself behind Crampton's right shoulder and assumes his professional tone.) Open, please. (Crampton opens his mouth. Valentine puts the mirror in, and examines his teeth.) Hm! You have broken that one. What a pity to spoil such a splendid set of teeth! Why do you crack nuts with them? (He withdraws the mirror, and comes forward to converse with Crampton.)

CRAMPTON. I've always cracked nuts with them: what else are they for? (Dogmatically.) The proper way to keep teeth good is to give them plenty of use on bones and nuts, and wash them every day with soap--- plain yellow soap.

VALENTINE. Soap! Why soap?

CRAMPTON. I began using it as a boy because I was made to; and I've used it ever since. And I never had toothache in my life.

VALENTINE. Don't you find it rather nasty?

CRAMPTON. I found that most things that were good for me were nasty. But I was taught to put up with them, and made to put up with them. I'm used to it now: in fact, I like the taste when the soap is really good.

VALENTINE (making a wry face in spite of himself). You seem to have been very carefully educated, Mr. Crampton.

CRAMPTON (grimly). I wasn't spoiled, at all events.

VALENTINE (smiling a little to himself). Are you quite sure?

CRAMPTON. What d'y' mean?

VALENTINE. Well, your teeth are good, I admit. But I've seen just as good in very self-indulgent mouths. (He goes to the ledge of cabinet and changes the probe for another one.)

CRAMPTON. It's not the effect on the teeth: it's the effect on the character.

VALENTINE (placably). Oh, the character, I see. (He recommences operations.) A little wider, please. Hm! That one will have to come out: it's past saving. (He withdraws the probe and again comes to the side of the chair to converse.) Don't be alarmed: you shan't feel anything. I'll give you gas.

CRAMPTON. Rubbish, man: I want none of your gas. Out with it. People were taught to bear necessary pain in my day.

VALENTINE. Oh, if you like being hurt, all right. I'll hurt you as much as you like, without any extra charge for the beneficial effect on your character.

wave
a finger
in his
face

CRAMPTON (rising and glaring at him). Young man: you owe me six weeks' rent.

VALENTINE. I do.

CRAMPTON. Can you pay me?

VALENTINE. No.

CRAMPTON (satisfied with his advantage). I thought not. How soon d'y' think you'll be able to pay me if you have no better manners than to make game of your patients? (He sits down again.)

VALENTINE. My good sir: my patients haven't all formed their characters on kitchen soap.

CRAMPTON (suddenly gripping him by the arm as he turns away again to the cabinet). So much the worse for them. I tell you you don't understand my character. If I could spare all my teeth, I'd make you pull them all out one after another to shew you what a properly hardened man can go through with when he's made up his mind to do it. (He nods at him to enforce the effect of this declaration, and releases him.)

VALENTINE (his careless pleasantry quite unruffled). And you want to be more hardened, do you?

CRAMPTON. Yes.

pause

VALENTINE (strolling away to the bell). Well, you're quite hard enough for me already--as a landlord. (Crampton receives this with a growl of grim humor. Valentine rings the bell, and remarks in a cheerful, casual way, whilst waiting for it to be answered.) Why did you never get married, Mr. Crampton? A wife and children would have taken some of the hardness out of you.

CRAMPTON (with unexpected ferocity). What the devil is that to you? (The parlor maid appears at the door.)

VALENTINE (politely). Some warm water, please. (She retires: and Valentine comes back to the cabinet, not at all put out by Crampton's rudeness, and carries on the conversation whilst he selects a forceps and places it ready to his hand with a gag and a drinking glass.) You were asking me what the devil that was to me. Well, I have an idea of getting married myself.

30

CRAMPTON (with grumbling irony). Naturally, sir, naturally. When a young man has come to his last farthing, and is within twenty-four hours of having his furniture distrained upon by his landlord, he marries. I've noticed that before. Well, marry; and be miserable.

VALENTINE. Oh, come, what do you know about it?

CRAMPTON. I'm not a bachelor.

VALENTINE. Then there is a Mrs. Crampton?

CRAMPTON (wincing with a pang of resentment). Yes---damn her!

VALENTINE (unperturbed). Hm! A father, too, perhaps, as well as a husband, Mr. Crampton?

CRAMPTON. Three children.

VALENTINE (politely). Damn them?--eh?

CRAMPTON (jealously). No, sir: the children are as much mine as hers. (The parlor maid brings in a jug of hot water.)

VALENTINE. Thank you. (He takes the jug from her, and brings it to the cabinet, continuing in the same idle strain) I really should like to know your family, Mr. Crampton. (The parlor maid goes out: and he pours some hot water into the drinking glass.)

CRAMPTON. Sorry I can't introduce you, sir. I'm happy to say that I don't know where they are, and don't care, so long as they keep out of my way. (Valentine, with a hitch of his eyebrows and shoulders, drops the forceps with a clink into the glass of hot water.) You needn't warm that thing to use on me. I'm not afraid of the cold steel. (Valentine stoops to arrange the gas pump and cylinder beside the chair.) What's that heavy thing?

VALENTINE. Oh, never mind. Something to put my foot on, to get the necessary purchase for a good pull. (Crampton looks alarmed in spite of himself. Valentine stands upright and places the glass with the forceps in it ready to his hand, chatting on with provoking indifference.) And so you advise me not to get married, Mr. Crampton? (He stoops to fit the handle on the apparatus by which the chair is raised and lowered.)

CRAMPTON (irritably). I advise you to get my tooth out and have done reminding me of my wife. Come along, man. (He grips the arms of the chair and braces himself.)

VALENTINE (pausing, with his hand on the lever, to look up at him and say). What do you bet that I don't get that tooth out without your feeling it?

CRAMPTON. Your six week's rent, young man. Don't you gammon me.

VALENTINE (jumping at the bet and winding him aloft vigorously). Done! Are you ready? (Crampton, who has lost his grip of the chair in his alarm at its sudden ascent, folds his arms: sits stiffly upright: and prepares for the worst. Valentine lets down the back of the chair to an obtuse angle.)

CRAMPTON (clutching at the arms of the chair as he falls back). Take care man. I'm quite helpless in this po----

VALENTINE (deftly stopping him with the gag, and snatching up the mouthpiece of the gas machine). You'll be more helpless presently. (He presses the mouthpiece over Crampton's mouth and nose, leaning over his chest so as to hold his head and shoulders well down on the chair. Crampton makes an inarticulate sound in the mouthpiece and tries to lay hands on Valentine, whom he supposes to be in front of him. After a moment his arms wave aimlessly, then subside and drop. He is quite insensible. Valentine, with an exclamation of somewhat preoccupied triumph, throws aside the mouthpiece quickly: picks up the forceps adroitly from the glass: and ---the curtain falls.)

END OF ACT I.

Act II

On the terrace at the Marine Hotel. It is a square flagged platform, with a parapet of heavy oil jar pilasters supporting a broad stone coping on the outer edge, which stands up over the sea like a cliff. The head waiter of the establishment, busy laying napkins on a luncheon table with his back to the sea, has the hotel on his right, and on his left, in the corner nearest the sea, the flight of steps leading down to the beach.

When he looks down the terrace in front of him he sees a little to his left a solitary guest, a middle-aged gentleman sitting on a chair of iron laths at a little iron table with a bowl of lump sugar and three wasps on it, reading the Standard, with his umbrella up to defend him from the sun, which, in August and at less than an hour after noon, is toasting his protended insteps. Just opposite him, at the hotel side of the terrace, there is a garden seat of the ordinary esplanade pattern. Access to the hotel for visitors is by an entrance in the middle of its facade, reached by a couple of steps on a broad square of raised pavement. Nearer the parapet there lurks a way to the kitchen, masked by a little trellis porch. The table at which the waiter is occupied is a long one, set across the terrace with covers and chairs for five, two at each side and one at the end next the hotel. Against the parapet another table is prepared as a buffet to serve from.

The waiter is a remarkable person in his way. A silky old man, white-haired and delicate looking, but so cheerful and contented that in his encouraging presence ambition stands rebuked as vulgarity, and imagination as treason to the abounding sufficiency and interest of the actual. He has a certain expression peculiar to men who have been extraordinarily successful in their calling, and who, whilst aware of the vanity of success, are untouched by envy.

THE GENTLEMAN at the iron table is not dressed for the seaside. He wears his London frock coat and gloves; and his tall silk hat is on the table beside the sugar bowl. The excellent condition and quality of these garments, the gold-rimmed folding spectacles through which he is reading the Standard, and the Times at his elbow overlaying the local paper, all testify to his respectability. He is about fifty, clean shaven, and close-cropped, with the corners of his mouth turned down purposely, as if he suspected them of wanting to turn up, and was

33

determined not to let them have their way. He has large expansive ears, cod colored eyes, and a brow kept resolutely wide open, as if, again, he had resolved in his youth to be truthful, magnanimous, and incorruptible, but had never succeeded in making that habit of mind automatic and unconscious. Still, he is by no means to be laughed at. There is no sign of stupidity or infirmity of will about him: on the contrary, he would pass anywhere at sight as a man of more than average professional capacity and responsibility. Just at present he is enjoying the weather and the sea too much to be out of patience; but he has exhausted all the news in his papers and is at present reduced to the advertisements, which are not sufficiently succulent to induce him to persevere with them.

THE GENTLEMAN (yawning and giving up the paper as a bad job). Waiterless

WAITER. Sir? (coming down C.)

THE GENTLEMAN. Are you quite sure Mrs. Clandon is coming back before lunch?

WAITER. Quite sure, sir. She expects you at a quarter to one, sir. (The gentleman, soothed at once by the waiter's voice, looks at him with a lazy smile. It is a quiet voice, with a gentle melody in it that gives sympathetic interest to his most commonplace remark; and he speaks with the sweetest propriety, neither dropping his aitches nor misplacing them, nor committing any other vulgarism. He looks at his watch as he continues) Not that yet, sir, is it? 12:43, sir. Only two minutes more to wait, sir. Nice morning, sir? *back behind the table.*

THE GENTLEMAN. Yes: very fresh after London.

WAITER. Yes, sir: so all our visitors say, sir. Very nice family, Mrs. Clandon's, sir.

THE GENTLEMAN. You like them, do you?

WAITER. Yes, sir. They have a free way with them that is very taking, sir, very taking indeed, sir: especially the young lady and gentleman.

THE GENTLEMAN. Miss Dorothea and Mr. Philip, I suppose.

WAITER. Yes, sir. The young lady, in giving an order, or the like of that, will say, "Remember, William, we came to this hotel on your account, having heard what a perfect waiter you are." The young gentleman will tell me that I remind him strongly of his father (the gentleman starts at this) and that he expects me to act by him as such. (Soothing, sunny cadence.) Oh, very pleasant, sir, very affable and pleasant indeed!

34

THE GENTLEMAN. You like his ~~father~~ [mother]! (He laughs at the notion.)

WAITER. Oh, we must not take what they say too seriously, sir. Of course, sir, if it were true, the young lady would have seen the resemblance, too, sir.

THE GENTLEMAN. Did she? [from the back] [Elizabeth the 1st] [liz]

WAITER. No, sir. She thought me like the bust of Shakespear in Stratford Church, sir. That is why she calls me ~~William,~~ sir. My real name is ~~Walter~~, sir. (He turns to go back to the table, and sees Mrs. Clandon coming up to the terrace from the beach by the steps.) Here is Mrs. Clandon, sir. (To Mrs. Clandon, in an unobtrusively confidential tone) Gentleman for you, ma'am.

MRS. CLANDON. We shall have two more gentlemen at lunch, ~~William.~~ [Elizabeth] [Boss]

WAITER. Right, ma'am. Thank you, ma'am. (He withdraws into the hotel. Mrs. Clandon comes forward looking round for her visitor, but passes over the gentleman without any sign of recognition.) [look around more]

THE GENTLEMAN (peering at her quaintly from under the umbrella). Don't you know me?

MRS. CLANDON (incredulously, looking hard at him) Are you Finch McComas?

McCOMAS. Can't you guess? (He shuts the umbrella; puts it aside; and jocularly plants himself with his hands on his hips to be inspected.)

MRS. CLANDON. I believe you are. (She gives him her hand. The shake that ensues is that of old friends after a long separation.) Where's your beard? [1 kiss on cheek,]

McCOMAS (with humorous solemnity). Would you employ a solicitor with a beard?

MRS. CLANDON (pointing to the silk hat on the table). Is that your hat?

McCOMAS. Would you employ a solicitor with a sombrero?

MRS. CLANDON. I have thought of you all these eighteen years with the beard and the sombrero. (She sits down on the garden seat. McComas takes his chair again.) Do you go to the meetings of the Dialectical Society still?

McCOMAS (gravely). I do not frequent meetings now.

35

MRS. CLANDON. Finch: I see what has happened. You have become respectable. *Sit down*

McCOMAS. Haven't you?

MRS. CLANDON. Not a bit.

McCOMAS. You hold to your old opinions still?

MRS. CLANDON. As firmly as ever.

McCOMAS. Bless me! And you are still ready to make speeches in public, in spite of your sex (Mrs. Clandon nods); to insist on a married woman's right to her own separate property (she nods again); to champion Darwin's view of the origin of species and John Stuart Mill's essay on Liberty (nod); to read Huxley, Tyndall and George Eliot (three nods); and to demand University degrees, the opening of the professions, and the parliamentary franchise for women as well as men?

MRS. CLANDON (resolutely). Yes: I have not gone back one inch; and I have educated Gloria to take up my work where I left it. That is what has brought me back to England: I felt that I had no right to bury her alive in Madeira--my St. Helena, Finch. I suppose she will be howled at as I was; but she is prepared for that.

McCOMAS. Howled at! My dear good lady: there is nothing in any of those views now-a-days to prevent her from marrying a bishop. You reproached me just now for having become respectable. You were wrong: I hold to our old opinions as strongly as ever. I don't go to church; and I don't pretend I do. I call myself what I am: a Philosophic Radical, standing for liberty and the rights of the individual, as I learnt to do from my master Herbert Spencer. Am I howled at? No: I'm indulged as an old fogey. I'm out of everything, because I've refused to bow the knee to Socialism.

MRS. CLANDON (shocked). Socialism.

McCOMAS. Yes, Socialism. That's what Miss Gloria will be up to her ears in before the end of the month if you let her loose here.

MRS. CLANDON (emphatically). But I can prove to her that Socialism is a fallacy.

McCOMAS (touchingly). It is by proving that, Mrs. Clandon, that I have lost all my young disciples. Be careful what you do: let her go her own way. (With some bitterness.) We're old-fashioned: the world thinks it has left us behind. There is only one place in all England where your opinions would still pass as advanced.

MRS. CLANDON (scornfully unconvinced). The Church, perhaps?

McCOMAS. No, the theatre. And now to business! Why have you made me come down here?

MRS. CLANDON. Well, partly because I wanted to see you---

McCOMAS (with good-humored irony). Thanks.

MRS. CLANDON. ---and partly because I want you to explain everything to the children. They know nothing; and now that we have come back to England, it is impossible to leave them in ignorance any longer. (Agitated.) Finch: I cannot bring myself to tell them. I--- (She is interrupted by the twins and Gloria. Dolly comes tearing up the steps, racing Philip, who combines a terrific speed with unhurried propriety of bearing which, however, costs him the race, as Dolly reaches her mother first and almost upsets the garden seat by the precipitancy of her arrival.) *Collapse in chair*

DOLLY (breathless). It's all right, mamma. The dentist is coming; and he's bringing his old man.

MRS. CLANDON. Dolly, dear: don't you see Mr. McComas? (Mr. McComas rises, smilingly.)

DOLLY (her face falling with the most disparagingly obvious disappointment). This! Where are the flowing locks?

PHILIP (seconding her warmly). Where the beard? ---the cloak? ---the poetic exterior?

DOLLY. Oh, Mr. McComas, you've gone and spoiled yourself. Why didn't you wait till we'd seen you?

McCOMAS (taken aback, but rallying his humor to meet the emergency). Because eighteen years is too long for a solicitor to go without having his hair cut.

GLORIA (at the other side of McComas). How do you do, Mr. McComas? (He turns; and she takes his hand and presses it, with a frank straight look into his eyes.) We are glad to meet you at last.

McCOMAS. Miss Gloria, I presume? (Gloria smiles assent, and releases his hand after a final pressure. She then retires behind the garden seat, leaning over the back beside Mrs. Clandon.) And this young gentleman?

PHILIP. I was christened in a comparatively prosaic mood. My name is---

DOLLY (completing his sentence for him declamatorily). "Norval. On the Grampian hills"---

PHILIP (declaiming gravely). "My father feeds his flock, a frugal swain"---

MRS. CLANDON (remonstrating). Dear, dear children: don't be silly. Everything is so new to them here, Finch, that they are in the wildest spirits. They think every Englishman they meet is a joke.

DOLLY. Well, so he is: it's not our fault.

PHILIP. My knowledge of human nature is fairly extensive, Mr. McComas; but I find it impossible to take the inhabitants of this island seriously.

McCOMAS. I presume, sir, you are Master Philip (offering his hand)?

PHILIP (taking McComas's hand and looking solemnly at him). I was Master Philip---was so for many years; just as you were once Master Finch. (He gives his hand a single shake and drops it; then turns away, exclaiming meditatively) How strange it is to look back on our boyhood! (McComas stares after him, not at all pleased.)

DOLLY (to Mrs. Clandon). Has Finch had a drink?

MRS. CLANDON (remonstrating). Dearest: Mr. McComas will lunch with us.

DOLLY. Have you ordered for seven? Don't forget the old gentleman.

MRS. CLANDON. I have not forgotten him, dear. What is his name?

DOLLY. Chalkstones. He'll be here at half past one. (To McComas.) Are we like what you expected?

MRS. CLANDON (changing her tone to a more earnest one). Dolly: Mr. McComas has something more serious than that to tell you. Children: I have asked my old friend to answer the question you asked this morning. He is your father's friend as well as mine: and he will tell you the story more fairly than I could. (Turning her head from them to Gloria.) Gloria: are you satisfied?

GLORIA (gravely attentive). Mr. McComas is very kind.

McCOMAS (nervously). Not at all, my dear young lady: not at all. At the same time, this is rather sudden. I was hardly prepared---er---

DOLLY (suspiciously). Oh, we don't want anything prepared.

38

PHILIP (exhorting him). Tell us the truth.

DOLLY (emphatically). Bald headed.

McCOMAS (nettled). I hope you intend to take what I have to say seriously.

PHILIP (with profound mock gravity). I hope it will deserve it, Mr. McComas. My knowledge of human nature teaches me not to expect too much.

MRS. CLANDON (remonstrating). Phil---

PHILIP. Yes, mother, all right. I beg your pardon, Mr. McComas: don't mind us.

DOLLY (in conciliation). We mean well.

PHILIP. Shut up, both.

(Dolly holds her lips. McComas takes a chair from the luncheon table; places it between the little table and the garden seat with Dolly on his right and Philip on his left; and settles himself in it with the air of a man about to begin a long communication. The Clandons match him expectantly.)

McCOMAS. Ahem! Your father---

DOLLY (interrupting). How old is he?

PHILIP. Sh!

MRS. CLANDON (softly). Dear Dolly: don't let us interrupt Mr. McComas.

McCOMAS (emphatically). Thank you, Mrs. Clandon. Thank you. (To Dolly.) Your father is fifty-seven.

DOLLY (with a bound, startled and excited). Fifty-seven! Where does he live?

MRS. CLANDON (remonstrating). Dolly, Dolly!

McCOMAS (stopping her). Let me answer that, Mrs. Clandon. The answer will surprise you considerably. He lives in this town. (Mrs. Clandon rises. She and Gloria look at one another in the greatest consternation.)

DOLLY (with conviction). I knew it! Phil: Chalkstones is our father.

39

McCOMAS. Chalkstones!

DOLLY. Oh, Crampstones, or whatever it is. He said I was like his mother. I knew he must mean his daughter.

PHILIP (very seriously). Mr. McComas: I desire to consider your feelings in every possible way: but I warn you that if you stretch the long arm of coincidence to the length of telling me that Mr. Crampton of this town is my father, I shall decline to entertain the information for a moment.

McCOMAS. And pray why?

PHILIP. Because I have seen the gentleman; and he is entirely unfit to be my father, or Dolly's father, or Gloria's father, or my mother's husband.

McCOMAS. Oh, indeed! Well, sir, let me tell you that whether you like it or not, he is your father, and your sister' father, and Mrs. Clandon's husband. Now! What have you to say to that!

DOLLY (whimpering). You needn't be so cross. Crampton isn't your father.

PHILIP. Mr. McComas: your conduct is heartless. Here you find a family enjoying the unspeakable peace and freedom of being orphans. We have never seen the face of a relative---never known a claim except the claim of freely chosen friendship. And now you wish to thrust into the most intimate relationship with us a man whom we don't know---

DOLLY (vehemently). An awful old man! (reproachfully) And you began as if you had quite a nice father for us.

McCOMAS (angrily). How do you know that he is not nice? And what right have you to choose your own father? (raising his voice.) Let me tell you, Miss Clandon, that you are too young to---

DOLLY (interrupting him suddenly and eagerly). Stop, I forgot! Has he any money?

McCOMAS. He has a great deal of money.

DOLLY (delighted). Oh, what did I always say, Phil?

PHILIP. Dolly: we have perhaps been condemning the old man too hastily. Proceed, Mr. McComas.

McCOMAS. I shall not proceed, sir. I am too hurt, too shocked, to proceed.

MRS. CLANDON (urgently). Finch: do you realize what is happening? Do you understand that my children have invited that man to lunch, and that he will be here in a few moments?

McCOMAS (completely upset).   What!   do you mean---am I to understand- --is it---

PHILIP (impressively).   Steady, Finch.   Think it out slowly and carefully. He's coming---coming to lunch.

GLORIA. Which of us is to tell him the truth? Have you thought of that?

MRS. CLANDON. Finch: you must tell him.

DOLLY Oh, Finch is no good at telling things. Look at the mess he has made of telling us.

McCOMAS. I have not been allowed to speak. I protest against this.

DOLLY (taking his arm coaxingly). Dear Finch: don't be cross.

MRS. CLANDON. Gloria: let us go in. He may arrive at any moment.

GLORIA (proudly). Do not stir, mother. I shall not stir. We must not run away.   ~~hand   on   her   Shoulder~~

MRS. CLANDON (delicately rebuking her).   My dear: we cannot sit down to lunch just as we are. We shall come back again. We must have no bravado. (Gloria winces, and goes into the hotel without a word.) Come, Dolly. (As she goes into the hotel door, the waiter comes out with plates, etc., for two additional covers on a tray.)

WAITER. Gentlemen come yet, ma'am?

MRS. CLANDON. Two more to come yet, thank you. They will be here, immediately. (She goes into the hotel. The waiter takes his tray to the service table.)

PHILIP. I have an idea. Mr. McComas: this communication should be made, should it not, by a man of infinite tact?

McCOMAS. It will require tact, certainly.

PHILIP   Good!   Dolly: whose tact were you noticing only this morning?

DOLLY (seizing the idea with rapture). Oh, yes, I declare! ~~William!~~

Elizabeth

PHILIP. The very man! (Calling) ~~William!~~ *One* *Elizabeth*

WAITER. Coming, sir. *Waitress*

McCOMAS (horrified). The waiter! Stop, stop! I will not permit this. I---

WAITER (presenting himself between Philip and McComas). Yes, sir. (McComas's complexion fades into stone grey; and all movement and expression desert his eyes. He sits down stupefied.)

PHILIP. ~~William~~ *Elizabeth*: you remember my request to you to regard me as your son?

WAITER (with respectful indulgence). Yes, sir. Anything you please, sir.

PHILIP. ~~William~~ *Elizabeth*: at the very outset of your career as my ~~father~~ *Parent*, a rival has appeared on the scene.

WAITER. Your ~~real~~ father, sir? Well, that was to be expected, sooner or later, sir, wasn't it? (Turning with a happy smile to McComas.) Is it you, sir?

McCOMAS (renerved by indignation). Certainly not. My children know how to behave themselves.

PHILIP. No, ~~William~~ *Elizabeth*: this gentleman was very nearly my father: he wooed my mother, but wooed her in vain.

McCOMAS (outraged). Well, of all the---

PHILIP. Sh! Consequently, he is only our solicitor. Do you know one Crampton, of this town?

WAITER. Cock-eyed Crampton, sir, of the Crooked Billet, is it?

PHILIP. I don't know. Finch: does he keep a public house?

McCOMAS (rising scandalized). No, no, no. Your father, sir, is a well-known yacht builder, an eminent man here.

WAITER (impressed). Oh, beg pardon, sir, I'm sure. A son of Mr. Crampton's! Dear me!

PHILIP. Mr. Crampton is coming to lunch with us.

WAITER (puzzled). Yes, sir. (Diplomatically.) Don't usually lunch with his family, perhaps, sir?

PHILIP (impressively). ~~William~~ *Elizabeth*: he does not know that we are his family. He has not seen us for eighteen years. He won't know us. (To emphasize the communication he seats himself on the iron table with a spring, and looks at the waiter with his lips compressed and his legs swinging.)

DOLLY. We want you to break the news to him, William.

WAITER. But I should think he'd guess when he sees your mother, miss. (Philip's legs become motionless at this elucidation. He contemplates the waiter raptly.)

DOLLY (dazzled). I never thought of that.

PHILIP. Nor I. (Coming off the table and turning reproachfully on McComas.) Nor you.

DOLLY. And you a solicitor!   *(Bess)?*

PHILIP. Finch: Your professional incompetence is appalling. William: your sagacity puts us all to shame. *Queen Elizabeth, Liz*

DOLLY You really are like ~~Shakespear~~, ~~William.~~

WAITER. Not at all, sir. Don't mention it, miss. Most happy, I'm sure, sir. (Goes back modestly to the luncheon table and lays the two additional covers, one at the end next the steps, and the other so as to make a third on the side furthest from the balustrade.)

PHILIP (abruptly). Finch: come and wash your hands. (Seizes his arm and leads him toward the hotel.)

McCOMAS. I am thoroughly vexed and hurt, Mr. Clandon---

PHILIP (interrupting him). You will get used to us. Come, Dolly. (McComas shakes him off and marches into the hotel. Philip follows with unruffled composure.)

DOLLY (turning for a moment on the steps as she follows them). Keep your wits about you, ~~William~~. There will be fire-works.

WAITER. Right, miss. You may depend on me, miss. (She goes into the hotel.) *Bess*

(Valentine comes lightly up the steps from the beach, followed doggedly by Crampton. Valentine carries a walking stick. Crampton, either because he is old and chilly, or with some idea of extenuating the unfashionableness of his reefer jacket, wears a light overcoat. He stops at the chair left by McComas in the middle of the terrace, and steadies himself for a moment by placing his hand on the back of it.)

43

CRAMPTON. Those steps make me giddy. (He passes his hand over his forehead.) I have not got over that infernal gas yet.

(He goes to the iron chair, so that he can lean his elbows on the little table to prop his head as he sits. He soon recovers, and begins to unbutton his overcoat. Meanwhile Valentine interviews the waiter.)

VALENTINE. Waiter! *ress*

WAITER (coming forward between them). Yes, sir.

VALENTINE. Mrs. Lanfrey Clandon.

WAITER (with a sweet smile of welcome). Yes, sir. We're expecting you, sir. That is your table, sir. Mrs. Clandon will be down presently, sir. The young lady and young gentleman were just talking about your friend, sir.

VALENTINE. Indeed!

WAITER (smoothly melodious). Yes, sire. Great flow of spirits, sir. A vein of pleasantry, as you might say, sir. (Quickly, to Crampton, who has risen to get the overcoat off.) Beg pardon, sir, but if you'll allow me (helping him to get the overcoat off and taking it from him). Thank you, sir. (Crampton sits down again; and the waiter resumes the broken melody.) The young gentleman's latest is that you're his father, sir.

CRAMPTON. What!

mother **WAITER**. Only his joke, sir, his favourite joke. Yesterday, I was to be his father. To-day, as soon as he knew you were coming, sir, he tried to put it up on me that you were his father, his long lost father- -- not seen you for eighteen years, he said.

CRAMPTON (startled). Eighteen years!

WAITER. Yes, sir. (With gentle archness.) But I was up to his tricks, sir. I saw the idea coming into his head as he stood there, thinking what new joke he'd have with me. Yes, sir: that's the sort he is: very pleasant, ve--ry off hand and affable indeed, sir. (Again changing his tempo to say to Valentine, who is putting his stick down *Crampton* against the corner of the garden seat) If you'll allow me, sir? (Taking Valentine's stick.) Thank you, sir. (Valentine strolls up to the luncheon table and looks at the menu. The waiter turns to Crampton and resumes his lay.) Even the solicitor took up the joke, although he was in a manner of speaking in my confidence about the young gentleman, sir. Yes, sir, I assure you, sir. You would never imagine what respectable professional gentlemen from London will do on an outing, when the sea air takes them, sir.

CRAMPTON. Oh, there's a solicitor with them, is there?

WAITER. The family solicitor, sir---yes, sir. Name of McComas, sir. (He goes towards hotel entrance with coat and stick, happily unconscious of the bomblike effect the name has produced on Crampton.)

CRAMPTON (rising in angry alarm). McComas! (Calls to Valentine.) Valentine! (Again, fiercely.) Valentine!! (Valentine turns.) This is a plant, a conspiracy. This is my family---my children--my infernal wife.

VALENTINE (coolly). On, indeed! Interesting meeting! (He resumes his study of the menu.)

CRAMPTON. Meeting! Not for me. Let me out of this. (Calling to the waiter.) Give me that coat.

WAITER. Yes, sir. (He comes back, puts Valentine's stick carefully down against the luncheon table; and delicately shakes the coat out and holds it for Crampton to put on.) I seem to have done the young gentleman an injustice, sir, haven't I, sir.

CRAMPTON. Rrrh! (He stops on the point of putting his arms into the sleeves, and turns to Valentine with sudden suspicion.) Valentine: you are in this. You made this plot. You---

VALENTINE (decisively). Bosh! (He throws the menu down and goes round the table to look out unconcernedly over the parapet.)

CRAMPTON (angrily). What d'ye--- (McComas, followed by Philip and Dolly, comes out. He vacillates for a moment on seeing Crampton.)

WAITER (softly--interrupting Crampton). Steady, sir. Here they come, sir. (He takes up the stick and makes for the hotel, throwing the coat across his arm. McComas turns the corners of his mouth resolutely down and crosses to Crampton, who draws back and glares, with his hands behind him. McComas, with his brow opener than ever, confronts him in the majesty of a spotless conscience.)

WAITER (aside, as he passes Philip on his way out). I've broke it to him, sir.

PHILIP. Invaluable William! (He passes on to the table.)

DOLLY (aside to the waiter). How did he take it?

WAITER (aside to her). Startled at first, miss; but resigned---very resigned, indeed, miss. (He takes the stick and coat into the hotel.)

McCOMAS (having stared Crampton out of countenance). So here you are, Mr. Crampton.

CRAMPTON. Yes, here--caught in a trap--a mean trap. Are those my children?

PHILIP (with deadly politeness). Is this our father, Mr. McComas?

McCOMAS. Yes--er--- (He loses countenance himself and stops.)

DOLLY (conventionally). Pleased to meet you again. (She wanders idly round the table, exchanging a smile and a word of greeting with Valentine on the way.)

PHILIP. Allow me to discharge my first duty as host by ordering your wine. (He takes the wine list from the table. His polite attention, and Dolly's unconcerned indifference, leave Crampton on the footing of the casual acquaintance picked up that morning at the dentist's. The consciousness of it goes through the father with so keen a pang that he trembles all over; his brow becomes wet; and he stares dumbly at his son, who, just conscious enough of his own callousness to intensely enjoy the humor and adroitness of it, proceeds pleasantly.) Finch: some crusted old port for you, as a respectable family solicitor, eh?

McCOMAS (firmly). Apollinaris only. I prefer to take nothing heating. (He walks away to the side of the terrace, like a man putting temptation behind him.)

PHILIP. Valentine---?

VALENTINE. Would Lager be considered vulgar?

PHILIP. Probably. We'll order some. Dolly takes it. (Turning to Crampton with cheerful politeness.) And now, Mr. Crampton, what can we do for you?

CRAMPTON. What d'ye mean, boy?

PHILIP. Boy! (Very solemnly.) Whose fault is it that I am a boy?

(Crampton snatches the wine list rudely from him and irresolutely pretends to read it. Philip abandons it to him with perfect politeness.)

DOLLY (looking over Crampton's right shoulder). The whisky's on the last page but one.

CRAMPTON. Let me alone, child.

DOLLY. Child! No, no: you may call me Dolly if you like; but you mustn't call me child. (She slips her arm through Philip's; and the two stand looking at Crampton as if he were some eccentric stranger.)

CRAMPTON (mopping his brow in rage and agony, and yet relieved even by their playing with him). McComas: we are--ha!--going to have a pleasant meal.

McCOMAS (pusillanimously). There is no reason why it should not be pleasant. (He looks abjectly gloomy.)

PHILIP. Finch's face is a feast in itself. (Mrs. Clandon and Gloria come from the hotel. Mrs. Clandon advances with courageous self-possession and marked dignity of manner. She stops at the foot of the steps to address Valentine, who is in her path. Gloria also stops, looking at Crampton with a certain repulsion.)

MRS. CLANDON. Glad to see you again, Mr. Valentine. (He smiles. She passes on and confronts Crampton, intending to address him with perfect composure; but his aspect shakes her. She stops suddenly and says anxiously, with a touch of remorse.) Fergus: you are greatly changed.

CRAMPTON (grimly). I daresay. A man does change in eighteen years.

MRS. CLANDON (troubled). I--I did not mean that. I hope your health is good.

CRAMPTON. Thank you. No: it's not my health. It's my happiness: that's the change you meant, I think. (Breaking out suddenly.) Look at her, McComas! Look at her; and look at me! (He utters a half laugh, half sob.)

PHILIP. Sh! (Pointing to the hotel entrance, where the waiter has just appeared.) Order before William! Bess

DOLLY (touching Crampton's arm warningly with her finger). Ahem! (The waiter goes to the service table and beckons to the kitchen entrance, whence issue a young waiter with soup plates, and a cook, in white apron and cap, with the soup tureen. The young waiter remains and serves: the cook goes out, and reappears from time to time bringing in the courses. He carves, but does not serve. The waiter comes to the end of the luncheon table next the steps.)

MRS. CLANDON (as they all assemble about the table). I think you have all met one another already to-day. Oh, no, excuse me. (Introducing) Mr. Valentine: Mr. McComas. (She goes to the end of the table nearest the hotel.) Fergus: will you take the head of the table, please.

47

CRAMPTON. Ha! (Bitterly.) The head of the table!

WAITER (holding the chair for him with inoffensive encouragement). This end, sir. (Crampton submits, and takes his seat.) Thank you, sir.

MRS. CLANDON. Mr. Valentine: will you take that side (indicating the side nearest the parapet) with Gloria? (Valentine and Gloria take their places, Gloria next Crampton and Valentine next Mrs. Clandon.) Finch: I must put you on this side, between Dolly and Phil. You must protect yourself as best you can. (The three take the remaining side of the table, Dolly next her mother, Phil next his father, and McComas between them. Soup is served.)

WAITER (to Crampton). Thick or clear, sir?

CRAMPTON (to Mrs. Clandon). Does nobody ask a blessing in this household?

PHILIP (interposing smartly). Let us first settle what we are about to receive. ~~William~~! Bess

WAITER. Yes, sir. (He glides swiftly round the table to Phil's left elbow. On his way he whispers to the young waiter) Thick.

PHILIP. Two small Lagers for the children as usual, ~~William~~; Bess and one large for this gentleman (indicating Valentine). Large Apollinaris for Mr. McComas.

WAITER. Yes, sir.

DOLLY. Have a six of Irish in it, Finch?

McCOMAS (scandalized). No--no, thank you.

PHILIP. Number 413 for my mother and Miss Gloria as before; and-- (turning enquiringly to Crampton) Eh?

CRAMPTON (scowling and about to reply offensively). I---

WAITER (striking in mellifluously). All right, sir. We know what Mr. Crampton likes here, sir. (He goes into the hotel.)

PHILIP (looking gravely at his father). You frequent bars. Bad habit! (The cook, accompanied by a waiter with a supply of hot plates, brings in the fish from the kitchen to the service table, and begins slicing it.)

CRAMPTON. You have learnt your lesson from your mother, I see.

48

MRS. CLANDON. Phil: will you please remember that your jokes are apt to irritate people who are not accustomed to us, and that your father is our guest to-day.

CRAMPTON (bitterly). Yes, a guest at the head of my own table. (The soup plates are removed.)

DOLLY (sympathetically). Yes: it's embarrassing, isn't it? It's just as bad for us, you know.

PHILIP. Sh! Dolly: we are both wanting in tact. (To Crampton.) We mean well, Mr. Crampton; but we are not yet strong in the filial line. (The waiter returns from the hotel with the drinks.) ~~William~~: come and restore good feeling. *Bess*

WAITER (cheerfully). Yes, sir. Certainly, sir. Small Lager for you, sir. (To Crampton.) Seltzer and Irish, sir. (To McComas.) Apollinaris, sir. (To Dolly.) Small Lager, miss. (To Mrs. Clandon, pouring out wine.) 413, madam. (To Valentine.) Large Lager for you, sir. (To Gloria.) 413, miss.

DOLLY (drinking). To the family!

PHILIP. (drinking). Hearth and Home! (Fish is served.)

McCOMAS (with an obviously forced attempt at cheerful domesticity). We are getting on very nicely after all.

DOLLY (critically). After all! After all what, Finch?

CRAMPTON (sarcastically). He means that you are getting on very nicely in spite of the presence of your father. Do I take your point rightly, Mr. McComas?

McCOMAS (disconcerted). No, no. I only said "after all" to round off the sentence. I---er---er---er---- *replies*

WAITER (tactfully). Turbot, sir?

McCOMAS (intensely grateful for the interruption). Thank you, waiter: thank you.

WAITER (sotto voce). Don't mention it, sir. (He returns to the service table.)

CRAMPTON (to Phil). Have you thought of choosing a profession yet? → *grunch*

PHILIP. I am keeping my mind open on that subject. ~~William!~~

Bess

49

WAITER. Yes, sir.

PHILIP. How long do you think it would take me to learn to be a really smart waiter?

WAITER. Can't be learnt, sir. It's in the character, sir. (Confidentially to Valentine, who is looking about for something.) Bread for the lady, sir? yes, sir. (He serves bread to Gloria, and resumes at his former pitch.) Very few are born to it, sir.

PHILIP. You don't happen to have such a thing as a son, yourself, have you?

WAITER. Yes, sir: oh, yes, sir. (To Gloria, again dropping his voice.) A little more fish, miss? you won't care for the joint in the middle of the day.

GLORIA. No, thank you. (The fish plates are removed.)

DOLLY. Is your son a waiter, too, William?

WAITER (serving Gloria with fowl). Oh, no, miss, he's too impetuous. He's at the Bar.

McCOMAS (patronizingly). A potman, eh?

WAITER (with a touch of melancholy, as if recalling a disappointment softened by time). No, sir: the other bar---your profession, sir. A Q.C., sir.

McCOMAS (embarrassed). I'm sure I beg your pardon.

WAITER. Not at all, sir. Very natural mistake, I'm sure, sir. I've often wished he was a potman, sir. Would have been off my hands ever so much sooner, sir. (Aside to Valentine, who is again in difficulties.) Salt at your elbow, sir. (Resuming.) Yes, sir: had to support him until he was thirty-seven, sir. But doing well now, sir: very satisfactory indeed, sir. Nothing less than fifty guineas, sir.

McCOMAS. Democracy, Crampton!---modern democracy!

WAITER (calmly). No, sir, not democracy: only education, sir. Scholarships, sir. Cambridge Local, sir. Sidney Sussex College, sir. (Dolly plucks his sleeve and whispers as he bends down.) Stone ginger, miss? Right, miss. (To McComas.) Very good thing for him, sir: he never had any turn for real work, sir. (He goes into the hotel, leaving the company somewhat overwhelmed by his son's eminence.)

VALENTINE. Which of us dare give that man an order again!

DOLLY. I hope he won't mind my sending him for ginger-beer.

CRAMPTON (doggedly). While he's a waiter it's his business to wait. If you had treated him as a waiter ought to be treated, he'd have held his tongue.

DOLLY. What a loss that would have been! Perhaps he'll give us an introduction to his son and get us into London society. (The waiter reappears with the ginger-beer.)

CRAMPTON (growling contemptuously). London society! London society!! You're not fit for any society, child.

DOLLY (losing her temper). Now look here, Mr. Crampton. If you think---

WAITER (softly, at her elbow). Stone ginger, miss.

DOLLY (taken aback, recovers her good humor after a long breath and says sweetly). Thank you, dear William. You were just in time. (She drinks.)

McCOMAS (making a fresh effort to lead the conversation into dispassionate regions). If I may be allowed to change the subject, Miss Clandon, what is the established religion in Madeira?

GLORIA. I suppose the Portuguese religion. I never inquired.

DOLLY. The servants come in Lent and kneel down before you and confess all the things they've done: and you have to pretend to forgive them. Do they do that in England, William?

WAITER. Not usually, miss. They may in some parts: but it has not come under my notice, miss. (Catching Mrs. Clandon's eye as the young waiter offers her the salad bowl.) You like it without dressing, ma'am: yes, ma'am, I have some for you. (To his young colleague, motioning him to serve Gloria.) This side, Jo. (He takes a special portion of salad from the service table and puts it beside Mrs. Clandon's plate. In doing so he observes that Dolly is making a wry face.) Only a bit of watercress, miss, got in by mistake. (He takes her salad away.) Thank you, miss. (To the young waiter, admonishing him to serve Dolly afresh.) Jo. (Resuming.) Mostly members of the Church of England, miss.

DOLLY. Members of the Church of England! What's the subscription?

CRAMPTON (rising violently amid general consternation). You see how my children have been brought up, McComas. You see it; you hear it. I call all of you to witness--- (He becomes inarticulate, and is about to strike his fist recklessly on the table when the waiter considerately takes away his plate.)

MRS. CLANDON (firmly).   Sit down, Fergus.   There is no occasion at all for this outburst.   You must remember that Dolly is just like a foreigner here.   Pray sit down.

CRAMPTON (subsiding unwillingly).   I doubt whether I ought to sit here and countenance all this.   I doubt it.

WAITER.   Cheese, sir; or would you like a cold sweet?

CRAMPTON (take aback).   What?   Oh!---cheese, cheese.

DOLLY.   Bring a box of cigarets, William. *Boss*

WAITER.   All ready, miss.   (He takes a box of cigarets from the service table and places them before Dolly, who selects one and prepares to smoke.   He then returns to his table for a box of vestas.)

CRAMPTON (staring aghast at Dolly).   Does she smoke?

DOLLY (out of patience).   Really, Mr. Crampton, I'm afraid I'm spoiling your lunch.   I'll go and have my cigaret on the beach.   (She leaves the table with petulant suddenness and goes down the steps. The waiter attempts to give her the matches; but she is gone before he can reach her.)

CRAMPTON (furiously).   Margaret: call that girl back.   Call her back, I say.

McCOMAS (trying to make peace).   Come, Crampton: never mind. She's her father's daughter: that's all.

MRS. CLANDON (with deep resentment).   I hope not, Finch.   (She rises: they all rise a little.)   Mr. Valentine: will you excuse me: I am afraid Dolly is hurt and put out by what has passed.   I must go to her.

CRAMPTON.   To take her part against me, you mean.

MRS. CLANDON (ignoring him).   Gloria: will you take my place whilst I am away, dear.   (She crosses to the steps.   Crampton's eyes follow her with bitter hatred.   The rest watch her in embarrassed silence, feeling the incident to be a very painful one.)

WAITER (intercepting her at the top of the steps and offering her a box of vestas).   Young lady forgot the matches, ma'am.   If you would be so good, ma'am.

MRS. CLANDON (surprised into grateful politeness by the witchery of his sweet and cheerful tones). Thank you very much. (She takes the matches and goes down to the beach. The waiter shepherds his assistant along with him into the hotel by the kitchen entrance, leaving the luncheon party to themselves.)

CRAMPTON (throwing himself back in his chair). There's a mother for you, McComas! There's a mother for you!

GLORIA (steadfastly). Yes: a good mother.

CRAMPTON. And a bad father? That's what you mean, eh?

VALENTINE (rising indignantly and addressing Gloria). Miss Clandon: I---

CRAMPTON (turning on him). That girl's name is Crampton, Mr. Valentine, not Clandon. Do you wish to join them in insulting me?

VALENTINE (ignoring him). I'm overwhelmed, Miss Clandon. It's all my fault: I brought him here: I'm responsible for him. And I'm ashamed of him.

CRAMPTON. What d'y' mean?

GLORIA (rising coldly). No harm has been done, Mr. Valentine. We have all been a little childish, I am afraid. Our party has been a failure: let us break it up and have done with it. (She puts her chair aside and turns to the steps, adding, with slighting composure, as she passes Crampton.) Good-bye, father.

(She descends the steps with cold, disgusted indifference. They all look after her, and so do not notice the return of the waiter from the hotel, laden with Crampton's coat, Valentine's stick, a couple of shawls and parasols, a white canvas umbrella, and some camp stools.)

CRAMPTON (to himself, staring after Gloria with a ghastly expression). Father! Father!! (He strikes his fist violently on the table.) Now---

WAITER (offering the coat). This is yours, sir, I think, sir. (Crampton glares at him; then snatches it rudely and comes down the terrace towards the garden seat, struggling with the coat in his angry efforts to put it on. McComas rises and goes to his assistance; then takes his hat and umbrella from the little iron table, and turns towards the steps. Meanwhile the waiter, after thanking Crampton with unruffled sweetness for taking the coat, offers some of his burden to Phil.) The ladies' sunshades, sir. Nasty glare off the sea to-day, sir: very trying to the complexion, sir. I shall carry down the camp stools myself, sir.

53

PHILIP.   You are old, ~~Father~~ ~~William~~; but you are the most considerate of men.   No: keep the sunshades and give me the camp stools (taking them).

WAITER (with flattering gratitude).   Thank you, sir.

PHILIP.   Finch: share with me (giving him a couple).   Come along. (They go down the steps together.)

VALENTINE (to the waiter).   Leave me something to bring down--one of these.   (Offering to take a sunshade.)

WAITER (discreetly).   That's the younger lady's, sir.   (Valentine lets it go.)   Thank you, sir.   If you'll allow me, sir, I think you had better have this.   (He puts down the sunshades on Crampton's chair, and produces from the tail pocket of his dress coat, a book with a lady's handkerchief between the leaves, marking the page.)   The eldest young lady is reading it at present.   (Valentine takes it eagerly.)   Thank you, sir. Schopenhauer, sir, you see.   (He takes up the sunshades again.)   Very interesting author, sir: especially on the subject of ladies, sir.   (He goes down the steps.   Valentine, about to follow him, recollects Crampton and changes his mind.)

VALENTINE (coming rather excitedly to Crampton).   Now look here, Crampton: are you at all ashamed of yourself?

CRAMPTON (pugnaciously).   Ashamed of myself!   What for?

VALENTINE.   For behaving like a bear.   What will your daughter think of me for having brought you here?

CRAMPTON.   I was not thinking of what my daughter was thinking of you.

VALENTINE.   No, you were thinking of yourself.   You're a perfect maniac.

CRAMPTON (heartrent).   She told you what I am---a father---a father robbed of his children.   What are the hearts of this generation like? Am I to come here after all these years---to see what my children are for the first time!   to hear their voices!---and carry it all off like a fashionable visitor; drop in to lunch; be Mr. Crampton---M i s t e r Crampton!   What right have they to talk to me like that?   I'm their father: do they deny that?   I'm a man, with the feelings of our common humanity: have I no rights, no claims?   In all these years who have I had round me?   Servants, clerks, business acquaintances.   I've had respect from them---aye, kindness.   Would one of them have spoken to me as that girl spoke?---would one of them have laughed at me as that boy was laughing at me all the time?   (Frantically.)   My own children!   M i s t e r Crampton!   My---

54

VALENTINE. Come, come: they're only children. The only one of them that's worth anything called you father.

CRAMPTON (wildly). Yes: "good-bye, father." Oh, yes: she got at my feelings---with a stab!

VALENTINE (taking this in very bad part). Now look here, Crampton: you just let her alone: she's treated you very well. I had a much worse time of it at lunch than you.

CRAMPTON. You!

VALENTINE (with growing impetuosity). Yes: I. I sat next to her; and I never said a single thing to her the whole time---couldn't think of a blessed word. And not a word did she say to me.

CRAMPTON. Well?

VALENTINE. Well? Well??? (Tackling him very seriously and talking faster and faster.) Crampton: do you know what's been the matter with me to-day? You don't suppose, do you, that I'm in the habit of playing such tricks on my patients as I played on you?

CRAMPTON. I hope not.

VALENTINE. The explanation is that I'm stark mad, or rather that I've never been in my real senses before. I'm capable of anything: I've grown up at last: I'm a Man; and it's your daughter that's made a man of me.

CRAMPTON (incredulously). Are you in love with my daughter?

VALENTINE (his words now coming in a perfect torrent). Love! Nonsense: it's something far above and beyond that. It's life, it's faith, it's strength, certainty, paradise---

CRAMPTON (interrupting him with acrid contempt). Rubbish, man! What have you to keep a wife on? You can't marry her.

VALENTINE. Who wants to marry her? I'll kiss her hands; I'll kneel at her feet; I'll live for her; I'll die for her; and that'll be enough for me. Look at her book! See! (He kisses the handkerchief.) If you offered me all your money for this excuse for going down to the beach and speaking to her again, I'd only laugh at you. (He rushes buoyantly off to the steps, where he bounces right into the arms of the waiter, who is coming up form the beach. The two save themselves from falling by clutching one another tightly round the waist and whirling one another around.)

WAITER (delicately). Steady, sir, steady.

VALENTINE (shocked at his own violence). I beg your pardon.

WAITER. Not at all, sir, not at all. Very natural, sir, I'm sure, sir, at your age. The lady has sent me for her book, sir. Might I take the liberty of asking you to let her have it at once, sir?

VALENTINE. With pleasure. And if you will allow me to present you with a professional man's earnings for six weeks--- (offering him Dolly's crown piece.)

so grateful

WAITER (as if the sum were beyond his utmost expectations). Thank you, sir: much obliged. (Valentine dashes down the steps.) Very high-spirited young gentleman, sir: very manly and straight set up.

CRAMPTON (in grumbling disparagement). And making his fortune in a hurry, no doubt. I know what his six weeks' earnings come to. (He crosses the terrace to the iron table, and sits down.)

WAITER (philosophically). Well, sir, you never can tell. That's a principle in life with me, sir, if you'll excuse my having such a thing, sir. (Delicately sinking the philosopher in the waiter for a moment.) Perhaps you haven't noticed that you hadn't touched that seltzer and Irish, sir, when the party broke up. (He takes the tumbler from the luncheon table, and sets if before Crampton.) Yes, sir, you never can tell. There was my son, sir! who ever thought that he would rise to wear a silk gown, sir? And yet to-day, sir, nothing less than fifty guineas, sir. What a lesson, sir!

CRAMPTON. Well, I hope he is grateful to you, and recognizes what he owes you.

WAITER. We get on together very well, very well indeed, sir, considering the difference in our stations. (With another of his irresistible transitions.) A small lump of sugar, sir, will take the flatness out of the seltzer without noticeably sweetening the drink, sir. Allow me, sir. (He drops a lump of sugar into the tumbler.) But as I say to him, where's the difference after all? If I must put on a dress coat to show what I am, sir, he must put on a wig and gown to show what he is. If my income is mostly tips, and there's a pretence that I don't get them, why, his income is mostly fees, sir; and I understand there's a pretence that he don't get them! If he likes society, and his profession brings him into contact with all ranks, so does mine, too, sir. If it's a little against a barrister to have a waiter for his father, sir, it's a little against a waiter to have a barrister for a son: many people consider it a great liberty, sir, I assure you, sir. Can I get you anything else, sir?

mother

CRAMPTON. No, thank you. (With bitter humility.) I suppose that's no objection to my sitting here for a while: I can't disturb the party on the beach here.

WAITER (with emotion). Very kind of you, sir, to put it as if it was not a compliment and an honour to us, Mr. Crampton, very kind indeed. The more you are at home here, sir, the better for us.

CRAMPTON (in poignant irony). Home!

WAITER (reflectively). Well, yes, sir: that's a way of looking at it, too, sir. I have always said that the great advantage of a hotel is that it's a refuge from home life, sir.

CRAMPTON. I missed that advantage to-day, I think.

WAITER. You did, sir, you did. Dear me! It's the unexpected that always happens, isn't it? (Shaking his head.) You never can tell, sir: you never can tell. (He goes into the hotel.)

CRAMPTON (his eyes shining hardly as he props his drawn, miserable face on his hands). Home! Home!! (He drops his arms on the table and bows his head on them, but presently hears someone approaching and hastily sits bolt upright. It is Gloria, who has come up the steps alone, with her sunshade and her book in her hands. He looks defiantly at her, with the brutal obstinacy of his mouth and the wistfulness of his eyes contradicting each other pathetically. She comes to the corner of the garden seat and stands with her back to it, leaning against the end of it, and looking down at him as if wondering at his weakness: too curious about him to be cold, but supremely indifferent to their kinship.) Well?

GLORIA. I want to speak with you for a moment.

CRAMPTON (looking steadily at her). Indeed? That's surprising. You meet your father after eighteen years; and you actually want to speak to him for a moment! That's touching: isn't it? (He rests his head on his hands, and looks down and away from her, in gloomy reflection.)

GLORIA. All that is what seems to me so nonsensical, so uncalled for. What do you expect us to feel for you---to do for you? What is it you want? Why are you less civil to us than other people are? You are evidently not very fond of us---why should you be? But surely we can meet without quarrelling.

CRAMPTON (a dreadful grey shade passing over his face). Do you realize that I am your father?

GLORIA. Perfectly.

CRAMPTON. Do you know what is due to me as your father?

GLORIA. For instance----?

CRAMPTON (rising as if to combat a monster). For instance! For instance!! For instance, duty, affection, respect, obedience---

GLORIA (quitting her careless leaning attitude and confronting him promptly and proudly). I obey nothing but my sense of what is right. I respect nothing that is not noble. That is my duty. (She adds, less firmly) As to affection, it is not within my control. I am not sure that I quite know what affection means. (She turns away with an evident distaste for that part of the subject, and goes to the luncheon table for a comfortable chair, putting down her book and sunshade.)

CRAMPTON (following her with his eyes). Do you really mean what you are saying?

GLORIA (turning on him quickly and severely). Excuse me: that is an uncivil question. I am speaking seriously to you; and I expect you to take me seriously. (She takes one of the luncheon chairs; turns it away from the table; and sits down a little wearily, saying) Can you not discuss this matter coolly and rationally?

CRAMPTON. Coolly and rationally! No, I can't. Do you understand that? I can't.

GLORIA (emphatically). No. That I c a n n o t understand. I have no sympathy with---

CRAMPTON (shrinking nervously). Stop! Don't say anything more yet; you don't know what you're doing. Do you want to drive me mad? (She frowns, finding such petulance intolerable. He adds hastily) No: I'm not angry: indeed I'm not. Wait, wait: give me a little time to think. (He stands for a moment, screwing and clinching his brows and hands in his perplexity; then takes the end chair from the luncheon table and sits down beside her, saying, with a touching effort to be gentle and patient) Now, I think I have it. At least I'll try.

GLORIA (firmly). You see! Everything comes right if we only think it resolutely out.

CRAMPTON (in sudden dread). No: don't think. I want you to feel: that's the only thing that can help us. Listen! Do you---but first---I forgot. What's your name? I mean you pet name. They can't very well call you Sophronia.

GLORIA (with astonished disgust). Sophronia! My name is Gloria. I am always called by it.

CRAMPTON (his temper rising again). Your name is Sophronia, girl: you were called after your aunt Sophronia, my sister: she gave you your first Bible with your name written in it.

GLORIA. Then my mother gave me a new name.

CRAMPTON (angrily). She had no right to do it. I will not allow this.

GLORIA. You had no right to give me your sister's name. I don't know her.

CRAMPTON. You're talking nonsense. There are bounds to what I will put up with. I will not have it. Do you hear that?

GLORIA (rising warningly). Are you resolved to quarrel?

CRAMPTON (terrified, pleading). No, no: sit down. Sit down, won't you? (She looks at him, keeping him in suspense. He forces himself to utter the obnoxious name.) Gloria. (She marks her satisfaction with a slight tightening of the lips, and sits down.) There! You see I only want to shew you that I am your father, my---my dear child. (The endearment is so plaintively inept that she smiles in spite of herself, and resigns herself to indulge him a little.) Listen now. What I want to ask you is this. Don't you remember me at all? You were only a tiny child when you were taken away from me; but you took plenty of notice of things. Can't you remember someone whom you loved, or (shyly) at least liked in a childish way? Come! someone who let you stay in his study and look at his toy boats, as you thought them? (He looks anxiously into her face for some response, and continues less hopefully and more urgently) Someone who let you do as you liked there and never said a word to you except to tell you that you must sit still and not speak? Someone who was something that no one else was to you--- who was your father.

GLORIA (unmoved). If you describe things to me, no doubt I shall presently imagine that I remember them. But I really remember nothing.

CRAMPTON (wistfully). Has your mother never told you anything about me?

GLORIA. She has never mentioned your name to me. (He groans involuntarily. She looks at him rather contemptuously and continues) Except once; and then she did remind me of something I had forgotten.

CRAMPTON (looking up hopefully). What was that?

GLORIA (mercilessly). The whip you bought to beat me with.

59

CRAMPTON (gnashing his teeth). Oh! To bring that up against me! To turn from me! When you need never have known. (Under a grinding, agonized breath.) Curse her!

GLORIA (springing up). You wretch! (With intense emphasis.) You wretch!! You dare curse my mother!

CRAMPTON. Stop; or you'll be sorry afterwards. I'm your father.

GLORIA. How I hate the name! How I love the name of mother! You had better go.

CRAMPTON. I---I'm choking. You want to kill me. Some---I--- (His voice stifles: he is almost in a fit.)

GLORIA (going up to the balustrade with cool, quick resourcefulness, and calling over to the beach). Mr. Valentine!

VALENTINE (answering from below). Yes.

GLORIA. Come here a moment, please. Mr. Crampton wants you. (She returns to the table and pours out a glass of water.)

CRAMPTON (recovering his speech). No: let me alone. I don't want him. I'm all right, I tell you. I need neither his help nor yours. (He rises and pulls himself together.) As you say, I had better go. (He puts on his hat.) Is that your last word?

GLORIA. I hope so. (He looks stubbornly at her for a moment; nods grimly, as if he agreed to that; and goes into the hotel. She looks at him with equal steadiness until he disappears, when she makes a gesture of relief, and turns to speak to Valentine, who comes running up the steps.)

VALENTINE (panting). What's the matter? (Looking round.) Where's Crampton?

GLORIA. Gone. (Valentine's face lights up with sudden joy, dread, and mischief. He has just realized that he is alone with Gloria. She continues indifferently) I thought he was ill; but he recovered himself. He wouldn't wait for you. I am sorry. (She goes for her book and parasol.)

VALENTINE. So much the better. He gets on my nerves after a while. (Pretending to forget himself.) How could that man have so beautiful a daughter!

GLORIA (taken aback for a moment; then answering him with polite but intentional contempt). That seems to be an attempt at what is called a pretty speech. Let me say at once, Mr. Valentine, that pretty

60

speeches make very sickly conversation. Pray let us be friends, if we are to be friends, in a sensible and wholesome way. I have no intention of getting married; and unless you are content to accept that state of things, we had much better not cultivate each other's acquaintance.

VALENTINE (cautiously). I see. May I ask just this one question? Is your objection an objection to marriage as an institution, or merely an objection to marrying me personally?

GLORIA. I do not know you well enough, Mr. Valentine, to have any opinion on the subject of your personal merits. (She turns away from him with infinite indifference, and sits down with her book on the garden seat.) I do not think the conditions of marriage at present are such as any self-respecting woman can accept.

VALENTINE (instantly changing his tone for one of cordial sincerity, as if he frankly accepted her terms and was delighted and reassured by her principles). Oh, then that's a point of sympathy between us already. I quite agree with you: the conditions are most unfair. (He takes off his hat and throws it gaily on the iron table.) No: what I want is to get rid of all that nonsense. (He sits down beside her, so naturally that she does not think of objecting, and proceeds, with enthusiasm) Don't you think it a horrible thing that a man and a woman can hardly know one another without being supposed to have designs of that kind? As if there were no other interests---no other subjects of conversation---as if women were capable of nothing better! turn back to him

GLORIA (interested). Ah, now you are beginning to talk humanly and sensibly, Mr. Valentine.

VALENTINE (with a gleam in his eye at the success of his hunter's guile). Of course!---two intelligent people like us. Isn't it pleasant, in this stupid, convention-ridden world, to meet with someone on the same plane---someone with an unprejudiced, enlightened mind?

GLORIA (earnestly). I hope to meet many such people in England.

VALENTINE (dubiously). Hm! There are a good many people here---nearly forty millions. They're not all consumptive members of the highly educated classes like the people in Madeira.

GLORIA (now full of her subject). Oh, everybody is stupid and prejudiced in Madeira---weak, sentimental creatures! I hate weakness; and I hate sentiment.

VALENTINE. That's what makes you so inspiring.

GLORIA (with a slight laugh). Am I inspiring?

VALENTINE Yes. Strength's infectious.

GLORIA. Weakness is, I know.

VALENTINE (with conviction). Y o u're strong. Do you know that you changed the world for me this morning? I was in the dumps, thinking of my unpaid rent, frightened about the future. When you came in, I was dazzled. (Her brow clouds a little. He goes on quickly.) That was silly, of course; but really and truly something happened to me. Explain it how you will, my blood got--- (he hesitates, trying to think of a sufficiently unimpassioned word) ---oxygenated: my muscles braced; my mind cleared; my courage rose. That's odd, isn't it? considering that I am not at all a sentimental man.

GLORIA (uneasily, rising). Let us go back to the beach.

VALENTINE (darkly---looking up at her). What! you feel it, too?

GLORIA. Feel what?

VALENTINE. Dread.

GLORIA. Dread!

VALENTINE. As if something were going to happen. It came over me suddenly just before you proposed that we should run away to the others.

GLORIA (amazed). That's strange---very strange! I had the same presentiment.

VALENTINE. How extraordinary! (Rising.) Well: shall we run away?

GLORIA. Run away! Oh, no: that would be childish. (She sits down again. He resumes his seat beside her, and watches her with a gravely sympathetic air. She is thoughtful and a little troubled as she adds) I wonder what is the scientific explanation of those fancies that cross us occasionally!

VALENTINE. Ah, I wonder! It's a curiously helpless sensation: isn't it?

GLORIA (rebelling against the word). Helpless?

VALENTINE. Yes. As if Nature, after allowing us to belong to ourselves and do what we judged right and reasonable for all these years, were suddenly lifting her great hand to take us---her two little children---by the scruff's of our little necks, and use us, in spite of ourselves, for her own purposes, in her own way.

GLORIA. Isn't that rather fanciful?

VALENTINE (with a new and startling transition to a tone of utter recklessness). I don't know. I don't care. (Bursting out reproachfully.) Oh, Miss Clandon, Miss Clandon: how could you? ↘ *Set down. desperate*

GLORIA. What have I done?

VALENTINE. Thrown this enchantment on me. I'm honestly trying to be sensible---scientific---everything that you wish me to be. But--- but--- oh, don't you see what you have set to work in my imagination?

GLORIA (with indignant, scornful sternness). I hope you are not going to be so foolish---so vulgar---as to say love.

VALENTINE (with ironical haste to disclaim such a weakness). No, no, no. Not love: we know better than that. Let's call it chemistry. You can't deny that there is such a thing as chemical action, chemical affinity, chemical combination---the most irresistible of all natural forces. Well, you're attracting me irresistibly---chemically.

GLORIA (contemptuously). Nonsense!

VALENTINE. Of course it's nonsense, you stupid girl. (Gloria recoils in outraged surprise.) Yes, stupid girl: t h a t's a scientific fact, anyhow. You're a prig---a feminine prig: that's what you are. (Rising.) Now I suppose you've done with me for ever. (He goes to the iron table and takes up his hat.) *watch ~~forward~~ cheaded*

GLORIA (with elaborate calm, sitting up like a High-school-mistress posing to be photographed). That shows how very little you understand my real character. I am not in the least offended. (He pauses and puts his hat down again.) I am always willing to be told of my own defects, Mr. Valentine, by my friends, even when they are as absurdly mistaken about me as you are. I have many faults---very serious faults---of character and temper; but if there is one thing that I am not, it is what you call a prig. (She closes her lips trimly and looks steadily and challengingly at him as she sits more collectedly than ever.)

VALENTINE (returning to the end of the garden seat to confront her more emphatically). Oh, yes, you are. My reason tells me so: my knowledge tells me so: my experience tells me so.

GLORIA. Excuse my reminding you that your reason and your knowledge and your experience are not infallible. At least I hope not.

VALENTINE. I must believe them. Unless you wish me to believe my eyes, my heart, my instincts, my imagination, which are all telling me the most monstrous lies about you.

GLORIA (the collectedness beginning to relax). Lies!

63

VALENTINE (obstinately). Yes, lies. (He sits down again beside her.) Do you expect me to believe that you are the most beautiful woman in the world?

GLORIA. That is ridiculous, and rather personal.

VALENTINE. Of course it's ridiculous. Well, that's what my eyes tell me. (Gloria makes a movement of contemptuous protest.) No: I'm not flattering. I tell you I don't believe it. (She is ashamed to find that this does not quite please her either.) Do you think that if you were to turn away in disgust from my weakness, I should sit down here and cry like a child?

GLORIA (beginning to find that she must speak shortly and pointedly to keep her voice steady). Why should you, pray?

VALENTINE (with a stir of feeling beginning to agitate his voice). Of course not: I'm not such an idiot. And yet my heart tells me I should--- my fool of a heart. But I'll argue with my heart and bring it to reason. If I loved you a thousand times, I'll force myself to look the truth steadily in the face. After all, it's easy to be sensible: the facts are the facts. What's this place? it's not heaven: it's the Marine Hotel. What's the time? it's not eternity: it's about half past one in the afternoon. What am I? a dentist---a five shilling dentist!

GLORIA. And I am a feminine prig.

VALENTINE. (passionately). No, no: I can't face that: I must have one illusion left---the illusion about you. I love you. (He turns towards her as if the impulse to touch her were ungovernable: she rises and stands on her guard wrathfully. He springs up impatiently and retreats a step.) Oh, what a fool I am!---an idiot! You don't understand: I might as well talk to the stones on the beach. (He turns away, discouraged.)

GLORIA (reassured by his withdrawal, and a little remorseful). I am sorry. I do not mean to be unsympathetic, Mr. Valentine; but what can I say?

VALENTINE (returning to her with all his recklessness of manner replaced by an engaging and chivalrous respect). You can say nothing, Miss Clandon. I beg your pardon: it was my own fault, or rather my own bad luck. You see, it all depended on your naturally liking me. (She is about to speak: he stops her deprecatingly.) Oh, I know you mustn't tell me whether you like me or not; but---

GLORIA (her principles up in arms at once). Must not! Why not! I am a free woman: why should I not tell you?

64

VALENTINE (pleading in terror, and retreating). Don't. I'm afraid to hear.

GLORIA (no longer scornful). You need not be afraid. I think you are sentimental, and a little foolish; but I like you.

VALENTINE (dropping into the iron chair as if crushed). Then it's all over. (He becomes the picture of despair.)

GLORIA (puzzled, approaching him). But why?

VALENTINE. Because liking is not enough. Now that I think down into it seriously, I don't know whether I like you or not.

GLORIA (looking down at him with wondering concern). I'm sorry.

VALENTINE (in an agony of restrained passion). Oh, don't pity me. Your voice is tearing my heart to pieces. Let me alone, Gloria. You go down into the very depths of me, troubling and stirring me---I can't struggle with it---I can't tell you--- *head in hands -*

GLORIA (breaking down suddenly). Oh, stop telling me what you feel: I can't bear it.

VALENTINE (springing up triumphantly, the agonized voice now solid, ringing, and jubilant). Ah, it's come at last---my moment of courage. (He seizes her hands: she looks at him in terror.) Our moment of courage! (He draws her to him; kisses her with impetuous strength; and laughs boyishly.) Now you've done it, Gloria. It's all over: we're in love with one another. (She can only gasp at him.) But what a dragon you were! And how hideously afraid I was!

PHILIP'S VOICE (calling from the beach). Valentine!

DOLLY'S VOICE. Mr. Valentine!

VALENTINE. Good-bye. Forgive me. (He rapidly kisses her hands, and runs away to the steps, where he meets Mrs. Clandon, ascending. Gloria, quite lost, can only start after him.)

MRS. CLANDON. The children want you, Mr. Valentine. (She looks anxiously around.) Is he gone?

VALENTINE (puzzled). He? (Recollecting.) Oh, Crampton. Gone this long time, Mrs. Clandon. (He runs off buoyantly down the steps.)

GLORIA (sinking upon the seat). Mother!

MRS. CLANDON (hurrying to her in alarm). What is it, dear?

GLORIA (with heartfelt, appealing reproach). Why didn't you educate me properly?

MRS. CLANDON (amazed). My child: I did my best.

GLORIA. Oh, you taught me nothing---nothing.

MRS. CLANDON. What is the matter with you?

GLORIA (with the most intense expression). Only shame---shame---shame. (Blushing unendurably, she covers her face with her hands and turns away from her mother.)

END OF ACT II.

Act III

The Clandon's sitting room in the hotel. An expensive apartment on the ground floor, with a French window leading to the gardens. In the centre of the room is a substantial table, surrounded by chairs, and draped with a maroon cloth on which opulently bound hotel and railway guides are displayed. A visitor entering through the window and coming down to this central table would have the fireplace on his left, and a writing table against the wall on his right, next the door, which is further down. He would, if his taste lay that way, admire the wall decoration of Lincrusta Walton in plum color and bronze lacquer, with dado and cornice; the ormolu consoles in the corners; the vases on pillar pedestals of veined marble with bases of polished black wood, one on each side of the window; the ornamental cabinet next the vase on the side nearest the fireplace, its centre compartment closed by an inlaid door, and its corners rounded off with curved panes of glass protecting shelves of cheap blue and white pottery; the bamboo tea table, with folding shelves, in the corresponding space on the other side of the window; the pictures of ocean steamers and Landseer's dogs; the saddlebag ottoman in line with the door but on the other side of the room; the two comfortable seats of the same pattern on the hearthrug; and finally, on turning round and looking up, the massive brass pole above the window, sustaining a pair of maroon rep curtains with decorated borders of staid green. Altogether, a room well arranged to flatter the occupant's sense of importance, and reconcile him to a charge of a pound a day for its use.

MRS. CLANDON sits at the writing table, correcting proofs. Gloria is standing at the window, looking out in a tormented revery.

The clock on the mantelpiece strikes five with a sickly clink, the bell being unable to bear up against the black marble cenotaph in which it is immured.

MRS. CLANDON. Five! I don't think we need wait any longer for the children. The are sure to get tea somewhere.

GLORIA (wearily). Shall I ring?

MRS. CLANDON. Do, my dear. (Gloria goes to the hearth and rings.) I have finished these proofs at last, thank goodness!

GLORIA (strolling listlessly across the room and coming behind her mother's chair). What proofs?

MRS. CLANDON The new edition of Twentieth Century Women.

GLORIA (with a bitter smile). There's a chapter missing.

MRS. CLANDON (beginning to hunt among her proofs). Is there? Surely not.

GLORIA. I mean an unwritten one. Perhaps I shall write it for you---when I know the end of it. (She goes back to the window.)

MRS. CLANDON. Gloria! More enigmas!

GLORIA. Oh, no. The same enigma.

MRS. CLANDON (puzzled and rather troubled; after watching her for a moment). My dear.

GLORIA (returning). Yes.

MRS. CLANDON. You know I never ask questions.

GLORIA (kneeling beside her chair). I know, I know. (She suddenly throws her arms about her mother and embraces her almost passionately.)

MRS. CLANDON. (gently, smiling but embarrassed). My dear: you are getting quite sentimental

GLORIA (recoiling). Ah, no, no. Oh, don't say that. Oh! (She rises and turns away with a gesture as if tearing herself.)

MRS. CLANDON (mildly). My dear: what is the matter? What--- (The waiter enters with the tea tray.)

WAITER (balmily). This was what you rang for, ma'am, I hope?

MRS. CLANDON. Thank you, yes. (She turns her chair away from the writing table, and sits down again. Gloria crosses to the hearth and sits crouching there with her face averted.)

WAITER (placing the tray temporarily on the centre table). I thought so, ma'am. Curious how the nerves seem to give out in the afternoon without a cup of tea. (He fetches the tea table and places it in front of Mrs. Cladon, conversing meanwhile.) the young lady and gentleman have just come back, ma'am: they have been out in a boat, ma'am. Very pleasant on a fine afternoon like this---very pleasant and

68

invigorating indeed. (He takes the tray from the centre table and puts it on the tea table.) Mr. McComas will not come to tea, ma'am: he has gone to call upon Mr. Crampton. (He takes a couple of chairs and sets one at each end of the tea table.)

GLORIA (looking round with an impulse of terror). And the other gentleman?

WAITER (reassuringly, as he unconsciously drops for a moment into the measure of "I've been roaming," which he sang as a boy.) Oh, he's coming, miss, he's coming. He has been rowing the boat, miss, and has just run down the road to the chemist's for something to put on the blisters. But he will be here directly, miss---directly. (Gloria, in ungovernable apprehension, rises and hurries towards the door.)

MRS. CLANDON. (half rising). Glo--- (Gloria goes out. Mrs. Clandon looks perplexedly at the waiter, whose composure is unruffled.)

what?

WAITER (cheerfully). Anything more, ma'am?

MRS. CLANDON. Nothing, thank you.

WAITER. Thank you, ma'am. (As he withdraws, Phil and Dolly, in the highest spirits, come tearing in. He holds the door open for them; then goes out and closes it.)

DOLLY (ravenously). Oh, give me some tea. (Mrs. Clandon pours out a cup for her.) We've been out in a boat. Valentine will be here presently.

PHILIP. He is unaccustomed to navigation. Where's Gloria?

MRS. CLANDON (anxiously, as she pours out his tea). Phil: there is something the matter with Gloria. Has anything happened? (Phil and Dolly look at one another and stifle a laugh.) What is it?

PHILIP (sitting down on her left). Romeo---

DOLLY (sitting down on her right). ---and Juliet.

PHILIP (taking his cup of tea from Mrs. Clandon). Yes, my dear mother: the old, old story. Dolly: don't take all the milk. (He deftly takes the jug from her.) Yes: in the spring---

DOLLY. ---a young man's fancy---

PHILIP. ---lightly turns to---thank you (to Mrs. Clandon, who has passed the biscuits) ---thoughts of love. It also occurs in the autumn. The young man in this case is---

Snap out

DOLLY. Valentine.

PHILIP. And his fancy has turned to Gloria to the extent of---

DOLLY. ---kissing her---

PHILIP. ---on the terrace---

DOLLY (correcting him). --on the lips, before everybody.

MRS. CLANDON (incredulously). Phil! Dolly! Are you joking? (They shake their heads.) Did she allow it?

nod in unison?

PHILIP. We waited to see him struck to earth by the lightning of her scorn;---

OTT

DOLLY. ---but he wasn't.

PHILIP. She appeared to like it.

DOLLY. As far as we could judge. (Stopping Phil, who is about to pour out another cup.) No: you've sworn off two cups.

MRS. CLANDON (much troubled). Children: you must not be here when Mr. Valentine comes. I must speak very seriously to him about this.

PHILIP. To ask him his intentions? What a violation of Twentieth Century principles!

sit back

DOLLY. Quite right, mamma: bring him to book. Make the most of the nineteenth century while it lasts.

PHILIP. Sh! Here he is. (Valentine comes in.)

VALENTINE Very sorry to be late for tea, Mrs. Clandon. (She takes up the tea-pot.) No, thank you: I never take any. No doubt Miss Dolly and Phil have explained what happened to me.

Dolly after

PHILIP (momentously rising). Yes, Valentine: we have explained.

DOLLY (significantly, also rising). We have explained very thoroughly.

PHILIP. It was our duty. (Very seriously.) Come, Dolly. (He offers Dolly his arm, which she takes. They look sadly at him, and go out gravely, arm in arm. Valentine stares after them, puzzled; then looks at Mrs. Clandon for an explanation.)

MRS. CLANDON (rising and leaving the tea table). Will you sit down, Mr. Valentine. I want to speak to you a little, if you will allow me. (Valentine sits down slowly on the ottoman, his conscience presaging a bad quarter of an hour. Mrs. Clandon takes Phil's chair, and seats herself deliberately at a convenient distance from him.) I must begin by throwing myself somewhat at your consideration. I am going to speak of a subject of which I know very little---perhaps nothing. I mean love.

VALENTINE. Love!

MRS. CLANDON. Yes, love. Oh, you need not look so alarmed as that, Mr. Valentine: I am not in love with you.

VALENTINE (overwhelmed). Oh, really, Mrs.--- (Recovering himself.) I should be only too proud if you were.

MRS. CLANDON. Thank you, Mr. Valentine. But I am too old to begin.

VALENTINE. Begin! Have you never---?

MRS. CLANDON. Never. My case is a very common one, Mr. Valentine. I married before I was old enough to know what I was doing. As you have seen for yourself, the result was a bitter disappointment for both my husband and myself. So you see, though I am a married woman, I have never been in love; I have never had a love affair; and to be quite frank with you, Mr. Valentine, what I have seen of the love affairs of other people has not led me to regret that deficiency in my experience. (Valentine, looking very glum, glances sceptically at her, and says nothing. Her color rises a little; and she adds, with restrained anger) You do not believe me?

VALENTINE (confused at having his thought read). Oh, why not? Why not?

MRS. CLANDON. Let me tell you, Mr. Valentine, that a life devoted to the Cause of Humanity has enthusiasms and passions to offer which far transcend the selfish personal infatuations and sentimentalities of romance. Those are not your enthusiasms and passions, I take it? (Valentine, quite aware that she despises him for it, answers in the negative with a melancholy shake of the head.) I thought not. Well, I am equally at a disadvantage in discussing those so-called affairs of the heart in which you appear to be an expert.

VALENTINE (restlessly). What are you driving at, Mrs. Clandon?

MRS. CLANDON. I think you know.

VALENTINE. Gloria?

MRS. CLANDON. Yes. Gloria.

VALENTINE (surrendering). Well, yes: I'm in love with Gloria. (Interposing as she is about to speak.) I know what you're going to say: I've no money.

MRS. CLANDON. I care very little about money, Mr. Valentine.

VALENTINE. Then you're very different to all the other mothers who have interviewed me.

MRS. CLANDON. Ah, now we are coming to it, Mr. Valentine. You are an old hand at this. (He opens his mouth to protest: she cuts him short with some indignation.) Oh, do you think, little as I understand these matters, that I have not common sense enough to know that a man who could make as much way in one interview with such a woman as my daughter, can hardly be a novice!

VALENTINE. I assure you---

MRS. CLANDON (stopping him). I am not blaming you, Mr. Valentine. It is Gloria's business to take care of herself; and you have a right to amuse yourself as you please. But---

VALENTINE (protesting). Amuse myself! Oh, Mrs. Clandon!

MRS. CLANDON (relentlessly). On your honor, Mr. Valentine, are you in earnest?

VALENTINE (desperately). On my honor I am in earnest. (She looks searchingly at him. His sense of humor gets the better of him; and he adds quaintly) Only, I always have been in earnest; and yet---here I am, you see!

MRS. CLANDON. This is just what I suspected. (Severely.) Mr. Valentine: you are one of those men who play with women's affections.

VALENTINE. Well, why not, if the Cause of Humanity is the only thing worth being serious about? However, I understand. (Rising and taking his hat with formal politeness.) You wish me to discontinue my visits.

MRS. CLANDON. No: I am sensible enough to be well aware that Gloria's best chance of escape from you now is to become better acquainted with you.

VALENTINE (unaffectedly alarmed). Oh, don't say that, Mrs. Clandon. You don't think that, do you?

MRS. CLANDON. I have great faith, Mr. Valentine, in the sound training Gloria's mind has had since she was a child.

VALENTINE (amazingly relieved). O-oh! Oh, that's all right. (He sits down again and throws his hat flippantly aside with the air of a man who has no longer anything to fear.)

MRS. CLANDON (indignant at his assurance). What do you mean?

VALENTINE (turning confidentially to her). Come: shall I teach you something, Mrs. Clandon?

MRS. CLANDON (stiffly). I am always willing to learn.

VALENTINE. Have you ever studied the subject of gunnery--- artillery- --cannons and war-ships and so on?

MRS. CLANDON. Has gunnery anything to do with Gloria?

VALENTINE. A great deal---by way of illustration. During this whole century, my dear Mrs. Clandon, the progress of artillery has been a duel between the maker of cannons and the maker of armor plates to keep the cannon balls out. You build a ship proof against the best gun known: somebody makes a better gun and sinks your ship. You build a heavier ship, proof against that gun: somebody makes a heavier gun and sinks you again. And so on. Well, the duel of sex is just like that.

MRS. CLANDON. The duel of sex!

VALENTINE. Yes: you've heard of the duel of sex, haven't you? Oh, I forgot: you've been in Madeira: the expression has come up since your time. Need I explain it? ---> _Patronising_

MRS. CLANDON (contemptuously). No.

VALENTINE. Of course not. Now what happens in the duel of sex? The old fashioned mother received an old fashioned education to protect her against the wiles of man. Well, you know the result: the old fashioned man got round her. The old fashioned woman resolved to protect her daughter more effectually---to find some armor too strong for the old fashioned man. So she gave her daughter a scientific education---your plan. That was a corker for the old fashioned man: he said it wasn't fair---unwomanly and all the rest of it. But that didn't do him any good. So he had to give up his old fashioned plan of attack--- you know- --going down on his knees and swearing to love, honor and obey, and so on.

MRS. CLANDON. Excuse me: that was what the woman swore.

Philosophical

73

VALENTINE. Was it? Ah, perhaps you're right---yes: of course it was. Well, what did the man do? Just what the artillery man does--- went one better than the woman---educated himself scientifically and beat her at that game just as he had beaten her at the old game. I learnt how to circumvent the Women's Rights woman before I was twenty- three: it's all been found out long ago. You see, my methods are thoroughly modern.

MRS. CLANDON (with quiet disgust). No doubt.

VALENTINE. But for that very reason there's one sort of girl against whom they are of no use.

MRS. CLANDON. Pray which sort?

VALENTINE. The thoroughly old fashioned girl. If you had brought up Gloria in the old way, it would have taken me eighteen months to get to the point I got to this afternoon in eighteen minutes. Yes, Mrs. Clandon: the Higher Education of Women delivered Gloria into my hands; and it was you who taught her to believe in the Higher Education of Women.

MRS. CLANDON (rising). Mr. Valentine: you are very clever.

VALENTINE (rising also). Oh, Mrs. Clandon!

MRS. CLANDON And you have taught me n o t h i n g. Good-bye.

VALENTINE (horrified). Good-bye! Oh, mayn't I see her before I go?

MRS. CLANDON. I am afraid she will not return until you have gone Mr. Valentine. She left the room expressly to avoid you. *enjoy that.*

VALENTINE (thoughtfully). That's a good sign. Good-bye. (He bows and makes for the door, apparently well satisfied.)

MRS. CLANDON (alarmed). Why do you think it a good sign?

VALENTINE (turning near the door). Because I am mortally afraid of her; and it looks as if she were mortally afraid of me. (He turns to go and finds himself face to face with Gloria, who has just entered. She looks steadfastly at him. He stares helplessly at her; then round at Mrs. Clandon; then at Gloria again, completely at a loss.)

GLORIA (white, and controlling herself with difficulty). Mother: is what Dolly told me true?

MRS. CLANDON. What did she tell you, dear?

74

GLORIA. That you have been speaking about me to this gentleman.

VALENTINE (murmuring). This gentleman! Oh!

MRS. CLANDON (sharply). Mr. Valentine: can you hold your tongue for a moment? (He looks piteously at them; then, with a despairing shrug, goes back to the ottoman and throws his hat on it.)

GLORIA (confronting her mother, with deep reproach). Mother: what right had you to do it?

MRS. CLANDON. I don't think I have said anything I have no right to say, Gloria.

VALENTINE (confirming her officiously). Nothing. Nothing whatever. (Gloria looks at him with unspeakable indignation.) I beg your pardon. (He sits down ignominiously on the ottoman.)

GLORIA. I cannot believe that any one has any right even to think about things that concern me only. (She turns away from them to conceal a painful struggle with her emotion.)

MRS. CLANDON. My dear, if I have wounded your pride---

GLORIA (turning on them for a moment). My p r i d e! My pride!! Oh, it's gone: I have learnt now that I have no strength to be proud of. (Turning away again.) But if a woman cannot protect herself, no one can protect her. No one has any right to try---not even her mother. I know I have lost your confidence, just as I have lost this man's respect;--- (She stops to master a sob.)

VALENTINE (under his breath). This man! (Murmuring again.) Oh!

MRS. CLANDON (in an undertone). Pray be silent, sir.

GLORIA (continuing). ---but I have at least the right to be left alone in my disgrace. I am one of those weak creatures born to be mastered by the first man whose eye is caught by them; and I must fulfill my destiny, I suppose. At least spare me the humiliation of trying to save me. (She sits down, with her handkerchief to her eyes, at the farther end of the table.)

VALENTINE (jumping up). Look here---

MRS. CLANDON. Mr. Va---

VALENTINE (recklessly). No: I will speak: I've been silent for nearly thirty seconds. (He goes up to Gloria.) Miss Clandon---

75

GLORIA (bitterly). Oh, not Miss Clandon: you have found that it is quite safe to call me Gloria.

VALENTINE. No, I won't: you'll throw it in my teeth afterwards and accuse me of disrespect. I say it's a heartbreaking falsehood that I don't respect you. It's true that I didn't respect your old pride: why should I? It was nothing but cowardice. I didn't respect your intellect: I've a better one myself: it's a masculine specialty. But when the depths stirred!---when my moment came!---when you made me brave!---ah, then, then, t h e n!

GLORIA. Then you respected me, I suppose.

VALENTINE. No, I didn't: I adored you. (She rises quickly and turns her back on him.) And you can never take that moment away from me. So now I don't care what happens. (He comes down the room addressing a cheerful explanation to nobody in particular.) I'm perfectly aware that I'm talking nonsense. I can't help it. (To Mrs. Clandon.) I love Gloria; and there's an end of it. *missed it.*

MRS. CLANDON (emphatically). Mr. Valentine: you are a most dangerous man. Gloria: come here. (Gloria, wondering a little at the command, obeys, and stands, with drooping head, on her mother's right hand, Valentine being on the opposite side. Mrs. Clandon then begins, with intense scorn.) Ask this man whom you have inspired and made brave, how many women have inspired him before (Gloria looks up suddenly with a flash of jealous anger and amazement); how many times he has laid the trap in which he has caught you; how often he has baited it with the same speeches; how much practice it has taken to make him perfect in his chosen part in life as the Duellist of Sex.

VALENTINE. This isn't fair. You're abusing my confidence, Mrs. Clandon. *whining*

MRS. CLANDON. Ask him, Gloria.

GLORIA (in a flush of rage, going over to him with her fists clenched). Is that true?

VALENTINE. Don't be angry---

GLORIA (interrupting him implacably). Is it true? Did you ever say that before? Did you ever feel that before---for another woman?

VALENTINE (bluntly). Yes. (Gloria raises her clenched hands.)

MRS. CLANDON (horrified, springing to her side and catching her uplifted arm). Gloria!! My dear! You're forgetting yourself. (Gloria, with a deep expiration, slowly relaxes her threatening attitude.)

76

VALENTINE. Remember: a man's power of love and admiration is like any other of his powers: he has to throw it away many times before he learns what is really worthy of it.

MRS. CLANDON. Another of the old speeches, Gloria. Take care.

VALENTINE (remonstrating). Oh!

GLORIA (to Mrs. Clandon, with contemptuous self-possession). Do you think I need to be warned now? (To Valentine.) You have tried to make me love you.

VALENTINE. I have.

GLORIA. Well, you have succeeded in making me hate you--- passionately.

VALENTINE (philosophically). It's surprising how little difference there is between the two. (Gloria turns indignantly away from him. He continues, to Mrs. Clandon) I know men whose wives love them; and they go on exactly like that.

MRS. CLANDON. Excuse me, Mr. Valentine; but had you not better go?

GLORIA. You need not send him away on my account, mother. He is nothing to me now; and he will amuse Dolly and Phil. (She sits down with slighting indifference, at the end of the table nearest the window.)

VALENTINE (gaily). Of course: that's the sensible way of looking at it. Come, Mrs. Clandon: you can't quarrel with a mere butterfly like me.

MRS. CLANDON. I very greatly mistrust you, Mr. Valentine. But I do not like to think that your unfortunate levity of disposition is mere shamelessness and worthlessness;---

GLORIA (to herself, but aloud). It is shameless; and it is worthless.

MRS. CLANDON. ---so perhaps we had better send for Phil and Dolly and allow you to end your visit in the ordinary way.

VALENTINE (as if she had paid him the highest compliment). You overwhelm me, Mrs. Clandon. Thank you. (The waiter enters.)

WAITER. Mr. McComas, ma'am.

MRS. CLANDON. Oh, certainly. Bring him in.

WAITER. He wishes to see you in the reception-room, ma'am.

sight lines ✓

MRS. CLANDON. Why not here?

WAITER. Well, if you will excuse my mentioning it, ma'am, I think Mr. McComas feels that he would get fairer play if he could speak to you away from the younger members of your family, ma'am.

MRS. CLANDON. Tell him they are not here.

WAITER. They are within sight of the door, ma'am; and very watchful, for some reason or other.

MRS. CLANDON (going). Oh, very well: I'll go to him.

WAITER (holding the door open for her). Thank you, ma'am. (She goes out. He comes back into the room, and meets the eye of Valentine, who wants him to go.) All right, sir. Only the tea-things, sir. (Taking the tray.) Excuse me, sir. Thank you sir. (He goes out.)

VALENTINE (to Gloria). Look here. You will forgive me, sooner or later. Forgive me now.

GLORIA (rising to level the declaration more intensely at him). Never! While grass grows or water runs, never, never, never!!!

VALENTINE (unabashed). Well, I don't care. I can't be unhappy about anything. I shall never be unhappy again, never, never, never, while grass grows or water runs. The thought of you will always make me wild with joy. (Some quick taunt is on her lips: he interposes swiftly.) No: I never said that before: that's new. ⟍ *move earlier*

GLORIA. It will not be new when you say it to the next woman.

VALENTINE. Oh, don't, Gloria, don't. (He kneels at her feet.) *one knee*

GLORIA. Get up. Get up! How dare you? (Phil and Dolly, racing, as usual, for first place, burst into the room. They check themselves on seeing what is passing. Valentine springs up.)

PHILIP (discreetly). I beg your pardon. Come, Dolly. (He turns to go.)

GLORIA (annoyed). Mother will be back in a moment, Phil. (Severely.) Please wait here for her. (She turns away to the window, where she stands looking out with her back to them.)

PHILIP (significantly). Oh, indeed. Hmhm!

DOLLY. Ahah!

PHILIP. You seem in excellent spirits, Valentine.

78

VALENTINE. I am. (Comes between them.) Now look here. You both know what's going on, don't you? (Gloria turns quickly, as if anticipating some fresh outrage.)

DOLLY. Perfectly. *Perch or desk*

VALENTINE. Well, it's all over. I've been refused---scorned. I'm only here on sufferance. You understand: it's all over. Your sister is in no sense entertaining my addresses, or condescending to interest herself in me in any way. (Gloria, satisfied, turns back contemptuously to the window.) Is that clear?

DOLLY. Serve you right. You were in too great a hurry.

PHILIP (patting him on the shoulder). Never mind: you'd never have been able to call your soul your own if she'd married you. You can now begin a new chapter in your life. *Stranger* *bitchy*

DOLLY. Chapter seventeen or thereabouts, I should imagine.

VALENTINE (much put out by this pleasantry). No: don't say things like that. That's just the sort of thoughtless remark that makes a lot of mischief.

DOLLY. Oh, indeed. Hmhm!

PHILIP. Ahah! (He goes to the hearth and plants himself there in his best head-of-the-family attitude.)

McCOMAS, looking very serious, comes in quickly with Mrs. Clandon, whose first anxiety is about Gloria. She looks round to see where she is, and is going to join her at the window when Gloria comes down to meet her with a marked air of trust and affection. Finally, Mrs. Clandon takes her former seat, and Gloria posts herself behind it. McComas, on his way to the ottoman, is hailed by Dolly.

DOLLY. What cheer, Finch?

McCOMAS (sternly). Very serious news from your father, Miss Clandon. Very serious news indeed. (He crosses to the ottoman, and sits down. Dolly, looking deeply impressed, follows him and sits beside him on his right.)

VALENTINE. Perhaps I had better go.

McCOMAS. By no means, Mr. Valentine. You are deeply concerned in this. (Valentine takes a chair from the table and sits astride of it, leaning over the back, near the ottoman.) Mrs. Clandon: your husband

79

demands the custody of his two younger children, who are not of age. (Mrs. Clandon, in quick alarm, looks instinctively to see if Dolly is safe.)

DOLLY (touched). Oh, how nice of him! He likes us, mamma.

McCOMAS. I am sorry to have to disabuse you of any such idea, Miss Dorothea.

DOLLY (cooing ecstatically). Dorothee-ee-ee-a! (Nestling against his shoulder, quite overcome.) Oh, Finch!

McCOMAS (nervously, moving away). No, no, no, no!

MRS. CLANDON (remonstrating). D e a r e s t Dolly! (To McComas.) The deed of separation gives me the custody of the children.

McCOMAS. It also contains a covenant that you are not to approach or molest him in any way.

MRS. CLANDON. Well, have I done so?

McCOMAS. Whether the behavior of your younger children amounts to legal molestation is a question on which it may be necessary to take counsel's opinion. At all events, Mr. Crampton not only claims to have been molested; but he believes that he was brought here by a plot in which Mr. Valentine acted as your agent.

VALENTINE. What's that? Eh?

McCOMAS. He alleges that you drugged him, Mr. Valentine.

VALENTINE. So I did. (They are astonished.)

McCOMAS. But what did you do that for?

DOLLY. Five shillings extra.

McCOMAS (to Dolly, short-temperedly). I must really ask you, Miss Clandon, not to interrupt this very serious conversation with irrelevant interjections. (Vehemently.) I insist on having earnest matters earnestly and reverently discussed. (This outburst produces an apologetic silence, and puts McComas himself out of countenance. He coughs, and starts afresh, addressing himself to Gloria.) Miss Clandon: it is my duty to tell you that your father has also persuaded himself that Mr. Valentine wishes to marry you---

VALENTINE (interposing adroitly). I do.

McCOMAS (offended). In that case, sir, you must not be surprised to find yourself regarded by the young lady's father as a fortune hunter.

VALENTINE. So I am. Do you expect my wife to live on what I earn? ten-pence a week!

McCOMAS (revolted). I have nothing more to say, sir. I shall return and tell Mr. Crampton that this family is no place for a father. (He makes for the door.)

MRS. CLANDON (with quiet authority). Finch! (He halts.) If Mr. Valentine cannot be serious, you can. Sit down. (McComas, after a brief struggle between his dignity and his friendship, succumbs, seating himself this time midway between Dolly and Mrs. Clandon.) You know that all this is a made up case---that Fergus does not believe in it any more than you do. Now give me your real advice---your sincere, friendly advice: you know I have always trusted your judgment. I promise you the children will be quiet.

McCOMAS (resigning himself). Well, well! What I want to say is this. In the old arrangement with your husband, Mrs. Clandon, you had him at a terrible disadvantage.

MRS. CLANDON. How so, pray?

McCOMAS. Well, you were an advanced woman, accustomed to defy public opinion, and with no regard for what the world might say of you.

MRS. CLANDON (proud of it). Yes: that is true. (Gloria, behind the chair, stoops and kisses her mother's hair, a demonstration which disconcerts her extremely.)

McCOMAS. On the other hand, Mrs. Clandon, your husband had a great horror of anything getting into the papers. There was his business to be considered, as well as the prejudices of an old-fashioned family.

MRS. CLANDON. Not to mention his own prejudices.

McCOMAS. Now no doubt he behaved badly, Mrs. Clandon---

MRS. CLANDON (scornfully). No doubt.

McCOMAS. But was it altogether his fault?

MRS. CLANDON. Was it mine?

McCOMAS (hastily). No. Of course not.

GLORIA (observing him attentively). You do not mean that, Mr. McComas. *harsh*

McCOMAS. My dear young lady, you pick me up very sharply. But let me just put this to you. When a man makes an unsuitable marriage (nobody's fault, you know, but purely accidental incompatibility of tastes); when he is deprived by that misfortune of the domestic sympathy which, I take it, is what a man marries for; when in short, his wife is rather worse than no wife at all (through no fault of his own, of course), is it to be wondered at if he makes matters worse at first by blaming her, and even, in his desperation, by occasionally drinking himself into a violent condition or seeking sympathy elsewhere?

MRS. CLANDON. I did not blame him: I simply rescued myself and the children from him.

McCOMAS. Yes: but you made hard terms, Mrs. Clandon. You had him at your mercy: you brought him to his knees when you threatened to make the matter public by applying to the Courts for a judicial separation. Suppose he had had that power over you, and used it to take your children away from you and bring them up in ignorance of your very name, how would you feel? what would you do? Well, won't you make some allowance for his feelings?---in common humanity.

MRS. CLANDON. I never discovered his feelings. I discovered his temper, and his--- (she shivers) the rest of his common humanity.

McCOMAS (wistfully). Women can be very hard, Mrs. Clandon.

VALENTINE. That's true.

GLORIA (angrily). Be silent. (He subsides.)

McCOMAS (rallying all his forces). Let me make one last appeal. Mrs. Clandon: believe me, there are men who have a good deal of feeling, and kind feeling, too, which they are not able to express. What you miss in Crampton is that mere veneer of civilization, the art of shewing worthless attentions and paying insincere compliments in a kindly, charming way. If you lived in London, where the whole system is one of false good-fellowship, and you may know a man for twenty years without finding out that he hates you like poison, you would soon have your eyes opened. There we do unkind things in a kind way: we say bitter things in a sweet voice: we always give our friends chloroform when we tear them to pieces. But think of the other side of it! Think of the people who do kind things in an unkind way---people whose touch hurts, whose voices jar, whose tempers play them false, who wound and worry the people they love in the very act of trying to conciliate them, and yet who need affection as much as the rest of us. Crampton has an abominable temper, I admit. He has no manners, no tact, no grace. He'll never be able to gain anyone's affection unless they will take his desire for it on trust. Is he to have none---not even pity---from his own flesh and blood?

82

DOLLY (quite melted). Oh, how beautiful, Finch! How nice of you!

PHILIP (with conviction). Finch: this is eloquence---positive eloquence.

DOLLY. Oh, mamma, let us give him another chance. Let us have him to dinner.

MRS. CLANDON (unmoved). No, Dolly: I hardly got any lunch. My dear Finch: there is not the least use in talking to me about Fergus. You have never been married to him: I have.

McCOMAS (to Gloria). Miss Clandon: I have hitherto refrained from appealing to you, because, if what Mr. Crampton told me to be true, you have been more merciless even than your mother.

GLORIA (defiantly). You appeal from her strength to my weakness!

McCOMAS. Not your weakness, Miss Clandon. I appeal from her intellect to your heart.

hand on shoulder.

GLORIA. I have learnt to mistrust my heart. (With an angry glance at Valentine.) I would tear my heart and throw it away if I could. My answer to you is my mother's answer. (She goes to Mrs. Clandon, and stands with her arm about her; but Mrs. Clandon, unable to endure this sort of demonstrativeness, disengages herself as soon as she can without hurting Gloria's feelings.)

McCOMAS (defeated). Well, I am very sorry---very sorry. I have done my best. (He rises and prepares to go, deeply dissatisfied.)

MRS. CLANDON. But what did you expect, Finch? What do you want us to do?

McCOMAS. The first step for both you and Crampton is to obtain counsel's opinion as to whether he is bound by the deed of separation or not. Now why not obtain this opinion at once, and have a friendly meeting (her face hardens)---or shall we say a neutral meeting? ---to settle the difficulty---here---in this hotel---to-night? What do you say?

MRS. CLANDON. But where is the counsel's opinion to come from?

McCOMAS. It has dropped down on us out of the clouds. On my way back here from Crampton's I met a most eminent Q.C., a man whom I briefed in the case that made his name for him. He has come down here from Saturday to Monday for the sea air, and to visit a relative of his who lives here. He has been good enough to say that if I can arrange a meeting of the parties he will come and help us with his opinion. Now do let us seize this chance of a quiet friendly family adjustment. Let me bring my friend here and try to persuade Crampton to come, too. Come: consent.

MRS. CLANDON (rather ominously, after a moment's consideration). Finch: I don't want counsel's opinion, because I intend to be guided by my own opinion. I don't want to meet Fergus again, because I don't like him, and don't believe the meeting will do any good. However (rising), you have persuaded the children that he is not quite hopeless. Do as you please.

McCOMAS (taking her hand and shaking it). Thank you, Mrs. Clandon. Will nine o'clock suit you?

hand bell

MRS. CLANDON. Perfectly. Phil: will you ring, please. (Phil rings the bell.) But if I am to be accused of conspiring with Mr. Valentine, I think he had better be present.

VALENTINE (rising). I quite agree with you. I think it's most important.

McCOMAS. There can be no objection to that, I think. I have the greatest hopes of a happy settlement. Good-bye for the present. (He goes out, meeting the waiter; who holds the door for him to pass through.)

MRS. CLANDON. We expect some visitors at nine, William. Can we have dinner at seven instead of half-past?

WAITER (at the door). Seven, ma'am? Certainly, ma'am. It will be a convenience to us this busy evening, ma'am. There will be the band and the arranging of the fairy lights and one thing or another, ma'am.

DOLLY. The fairy lights!

PHILIP. The band! William: what mean you?

WAITER. The fancy ball, miss---

DOLLY and PHILIP (simultaneously rushing to him). Fancy ball!

WAITER. Oh, yes, sir. Given by the regatta committee for the benefit of the Life-boat, sir. (To Mrs. Clandon.) We often have them, ma'am: Chinese lanterns in the garden, ma'am: very bright and pleasant, very gay and innocent indeed. (To Phil.) Tickets downstairs at the office, sir, five shillings: ladies half price if accompanied by a gentleman.

PHILIP (seizing his arm to drag him off). To the office, William!

84

DOLLY (breathlessly, seizing his other arm). Quick, before they're all sold. (They rush him out of the room between them.)

MRS. CLANDON. What on earth are they going to do? (Going out.) I really must go and stop this--- (She follows them, speaking as she disappears. Gloria stares coolly at Valentine, and then deliberately looks at her watch.)

VALENTINE. I understand. I've stayed too long. I'm going.

GLORIA (with disdainful punctiliousness). I owe you some apology, Mr. Valentine. I am conscious of having spoken somewhat sharply--- perhaps rudely---to you.

VALENTINE. Not at all.

GLORIA. My only excuse is that it is very difficult to give consideration and respect when there is no dignity of character on the other side to command it.

VALENTINE (prosaically). How is a man to look dignified when he's infatuated?

GLORIA (effectually unstilted). Don't say those things to me. I forbid you. They are insults.

VALENTINE. No: they're only follies. I can't help them.

GLORIA. If you were really in love, it would not make you foolish: it would give you dignity---earnestness---even beauty.

VALENTINE. Do you really think it would make me beautiful? (She turns her back on him with the coldest contempt.) Ah, you see you're not in earnest. Love can't give any man new gifts. It can only heighten the gifts he was born with.

GLORIA (sweeping round at him again). What gifts were you born with, pray?

VALENTINE. Lightness of heart.

GLORIA. And lightness of head, and lightness of faith, and lightness of everything that makes a man.

VALENTINE. Yes, the whole world is like a feather dancing in the light now; and Gloria is the sun. (She rears her head angrily.) I beg your pardon: I'm off. Back at nine. Good-bye. (He runs off gaily, leaving her standing in the middle of the room staring after him.)

END OF ACT III

Act IV

The same room. Nine o'clock. Nobody present. The lamps are lighted; but the curtains are not drawn. The window stands wide open; and strings of Chinese lanterns are glowing among the trees outside, with the starry sky beyond. The band is playing dance-music in the garden, drowning the sound of the sea.

The waiter enters, shewing in Crampton and McComas. Crampton looks cowed and anxious. He sits down wearily and timidly on the ottoman.

WAITER. The ladies have gone for a turn through the grounds to see the fancy dresses, sir. If you will be so good as to take seats, gentlemen, I shall tell them. (He is about to go into the garden through the window when McComas stops him.)

McCOMAS. One moment. If another gentleman comes, shew him in without any delay: we are expecting him.

WAITER. Right, sir. What name, sir?

McCOMAS. Boon. Mr. Boon. He is a stranger to Mrs. Clandon; so he may give you a card. If so, the name is spelt B.O.H.U.N. You will not forget.

WAITER (smiling). You may depend on me for that, sir. My own name is Boon, sir, though I am best known down here as Balmy Walters, sir. By rights I should spell it with the aitch you, sir; but I think it best not to take that liberty, sir. There is Norman blood in it, sir; and Norman blood is not a recommendation to a waiter.

McCOMAS. Well, well: "True hearts are more than coronets, and simple faith than Norman blood."

WAITER. That depends a good deal on one's station in life, sir. If you were a waiter, sir, you'd find that simple faith would leave you just as short as Norman blood. I find it best to spell myself B. double-O.N., and to keep my wits pretty sharp about me. But I'm taking up your time, sir. You'll excuse me, sir: your own fault for being so affable, sir.

87

I'll tell the ladies you're here, sir. (He goes out into the garden through the window.)

McCOMAS. Crampton: I can depend on you, can't I?

CRAMPTON. Yes, yes. I'll be quiet. I'll be patient. I'll do my best.

McCOMAS. Remember: I've not given you away. I've told them it was all their fault.

CRAMPTON. You told me that it was all my fault.

McCOMAS. I told you the truth.

CRAMPTON (plaintively). If they will only be fair to me!

McCOMAS. My dear Crampton, they won't be fair to you: it's not to be expected from them at their age. If you're going to make impossible conditions of this kind, we may as well go back home at once.

CRAMPTON. But surely I have a right---

McCOMAS (intolerantly). You won't get your rights. Now, once for all, Crampton, did your promises of good behavior only mean that you won't complain if there's nothing to complain of? Because, if so--- (He moves as if to go.)

CRAMPTON (miserably). No, no: let me alone, can't you? I've been bullied enough: I've been tormented enough. I tell you I'll do my best. But if that girl begins to talk to me like that and to look at me like--- (He breaks off and buries his head in his hands.)

McCOMAS (relenting). There, there: it'll be all right, if you will only bear and forbear. Come, pull yourself together: there's someone coming. (Crampton, too dejected to care much, hardly changes his attitude. Gloria enters from the garden; McComas goes to meet her at the window; so that he can speak to her without being heard by Crampton.) There he is, Miss Clandon. Be kind to him. I'll leave you with him for a moment. (He goes into the garden. Gloria comes in and strolls coolly down the middle of the room.)

CRAMPTON (looking round in alarm). Where's McComas?

GLORIA (listlessly, but not unsympathetically). Gone out---to leave us together. Delicacy on his part, I suppose. (She stops beside him and looks quaintly down at him.) Well, father?

CRAMPTON (a quaint jocosity breaking through his forlornness). Well, daughter? (They look at one another for a moment, with a melancholy sense of humor.)

GLORIA. Shake hands. (They shake hands.)

CRAMPTON (holding her hand). My dear: I'm afraid I spoke very improperly of your mother this afternoon.

GLORIA. Oh, don't apologize. I was very high and mighty myself; but I've come down since: oh, yes: I've been brought down. (She sits on the floor beside his chair.)

CRAMPTON. What has happened to you, my child?

GLORIA. Oh, never mind. I was playing the part of my mother's daughter then; but I'm not: I'm my father's daughter. (Looking at him funnily.) That's a come down, isn't it?

CRAMPTON (angry). What! (Her odd expression does not alter. He surrenders.) Well, yes, my dear: I suppose it is, I suppose it is. (She nods sympathetically.) I'm afraid I'm sometimes a little irritable; but I know what's right and reasonable all the time, even when I don't act on it. Can you believe that?

GLORIA. Believe it! Why, that's myself---myself all over. I know what's right and dignified and strong and noble, just as well as she does; but oh, the things I do! the things I do! the things I let other people do!!

CRAMPTON (a little grudgingly in spite of himself). As well as she does? You mean your mother?

GLORIA (quickly). Yes, mother. (She turns to him on her knees and seizes his hands.) Now listen. No treason to her: no word, no thought against her. She is our superior---yours and mine---high heavens above us. Is that agreed?

CRAMPTON. Yes, yes. Just as you please, my dear.

GLORIA (not satisfied, letting go his hands and drawing back from him). You don't like her?

CRAMPTON. My child: you haven't been married to her. I have. (She raises herself slowly to her feet, looking at him with growing coldness.) She did me a great wrong in marrying me without really caring for me. But after that, the wrong was all on my side, I dare say. (He offers her his hand again.)

GLORIA (taking it firmly and warningly). Take care. That's a dangerous subject. My feelings---my miserable, cowardly, womanly feelings---may be on your side; but my conscience is on hers.

CRAMPTON. I'm very well content with that division, my dear. Thank you. (Valentine arrives. Gloria immediately becomes deliberately haughty.)

VALENTINE. Excuse me; but it's impossible to find a servant to announce one: even the never failing William seems to be at the ball. I should have gone myself; only I haven't five shillings to buy a ticket. How are you getting on, Crampton? Better, eh?

CRAMPTON. I am myself again, Mr. Valentine, no thanks to you.

VALENTINE. Look at this ungrateful parent of yours, Miss Clandon! I saved him from an excruciating pang; and he reviles me!

↗ walk away

GLORIA (coldly). I am sorry my mother is not here to receive you, Mr. Valentine. It is not quite nine o'clock; and the gentleman of whom Mr. McComas spoke, the lawyer, is not yet come.

VALENTINE. Oh, yes, he is. I've met him and talked to him. (With gay malice.) You'll like him, Miss Clandon: he's the very incarnation of intellect. You can hear his mind working.

GLORIA (ignoring the jibe). Where is he?

VALENTINE. Bought a false nose and gone into the fancy ball.

CRAMPTON (crustily, looking at his watch). It seems that everybody has gone to this fancy ball instead of keeping to our appointment here.

VALENTINE. Oh, he'll come all right enough: that was half an hour ago. I didn't like to borrow five shillings from him and go in with him; so I joined the mob and looked through the railings until Miss Clandon disappeared into the hotel through the window.

GLORIA. So it has come to this, that you follow me about in public to stare at me.

VALENTINE. Yes: somebody ought to chain me up.

GLORIA turns her back on him and goes to the fireplace. He takes the snub very philosophically, and goes to the opposite side of the room. The waiter appears at the window, ushering in Mrs. Clandon and McComas.

MRS. CLANDON (hurrying in). I am so sorry to have kept you waiting.

A grotesquely majestic stranger, in a domino and false nose, with goggles, appears at the window.

WAITER (to the stranger). Beg pardon, sir; but this is a private apartment, sir. If you will allow me, sir, I will shew you to the American bar and supper rooms, sir. This way, sir.

He goes into the gardens, leading the way under the impression that the stranger is following him. The majestic one, however, comes straight into the room to the end of the table, where, with impressive deliberation, he takes off the false nose and then the domino, rolling up the nose into the domino and throwing the bundle on the table like a champion throwing down his glove. He is now seen to be a stout, tall man between forty and fifty, clean shaven, with a midnight oil pallor emphasized by stiff black hair, cropped short and oiled, and eyebrows like early Victorian horsehair upholstery. Physically and spiritually, a coarsened man: in cunning and logic, a ruthlessly sharpened one. His bearing as he enters is sufficiently imposing and disquieting; but when he speaks, his powerful, menacing voice, impressively articulated speech, strong inexorable manner, and a terrifying power of intensely critical listening raise the impression produced by him to absolute tremendousness.

THE STRANGER. My name is Bohun. (General awe.) Have I the honor of addressing Mrs. Clandon? (Mrs. Clandon bows. Bohun bows.) Miss Clandon? (Gloria bows. Bohun bows.) Mr. Clandon?

CRAMPTON (insisting on his rightful name as angrily as he dares). My name is Crampton, sir.

BOHUN. Oh, indeed. (Passing him over without further notice and turning to Valentine.) Are you Mr. Clandon?

VALENTINE (making it a point of honor not to be impressed by him). Do I look like it? My name is Valentine. I did the drugging.

BOHUN. Ah, quite so. Then Mr. Clandon has not yet arrived?

WAITER (entering anxiously through the window). Beg pardon, ma'am; but can you tell me what became of that--- (He recognizes Bohun, and loses all his self-possession. Bohun waits rigidly for him to pull himself together. After a pathetic exhibition of confusion, he recovers himself sufficiently to address Bohun weakly but coherently.) Beg pardon, sir, I'm sure, sir. Was---was it you, sir?

BOHUN (ruthlessly). It was I.

WAITER (brokenly). Yes, sir. (Unable to restrain his tears.) You in a false nose, Walter! (He sinks faintly into a chair at the table.) I beg pardon, ma'am, I'm sure. A little giddiness---

BOHUN (commandingly). You will excuse him, Mrs. Clandon, when I inform you that he is my father.

WAITER (heartbroken). Oh, no, no, Walter. A waiter for your father on the top of a false nose! What will they think of you?

MRS. CLANDON (going to the waiter's chair in her kindest manner). I am delighted to hear it, Mr. Bohun. Your father has been an excellent friend to us since we came here. (Bohun bows gravely.)

WAITER (shaking his head). Oh, no, ma'am. It's very kind of you--- very ladylike and affable indeed, ma'am; but I should feel at a great disadvantage off my own proper footing. Never mind my being the gentleman's father, ma'am: it is only the accident of birth after all, ma'am. (He gets up feebly.) You'll all excuse me, I'm sure, having interrupted your business. (He begins to make his way along the table, supporting himself from chair to chair, with his eye on the door.)

BOHUN. One moment. (The waiter stops, with a sinking heart.) My father was a witness of what passed to-day, was he not, Mrs. Clandon?

MRS. CLANDON. Yes, most of it, I think.

BOHUN. In that case we shall want him.

WAITER (pleading). I hope it may not be necessary, sir. Busy evening for me, sir, with that ball: very busy evening indeed, sir.

BOHUN (inexorably). We shall want you.

MRS. CLANDON (politely). Sit down, won't you?

WAITER (earnestly). Oh, if you please, ma'am, I really must draw the line at sitting down. I couldn't let myself be seen doing such a thing, ma'am: thank you, I am sure, all the same. (He looks round from face to face wretchedly, with an expression that would melt a heart of stone.)

GLORIA. Don't let us waste time. William only wants to go on taking care of us. I should like a cup of coffee.

WAITER (brightening perceptibly). Coffee, miss? (He gives a little gasp of hope.) Certainly, miss. Thank you, miss: very timely, miss, very thoughtful and considerate indeed. (To Mrs. Clandon, timidly but expectantly.) Anything for you, ma'am?

MRS. CLANDON Er---oh, yes: it's so hot, I think we might have a jug of claret cup.

WAITER (beaming). Claret cup, ma'am! Certainly, ma'am.

GLORIA Oh, well I'll have a claret cup instead of coffee. Put some cucumber in it.

WAITER (delighted). Cucumber, miss! yes, miss. (To Bohun.) Anything special for you, sir? You don't like cucumber, sir.

BOHUN. If Mrs. Clandon will allow me---syphon---Scotch.

WAITER. Right, sir. (To Crampton.) Irish for you, sir, I think, sir? (Crampton assents with a grunt. The waiter looks enquiringly at Valentine.)

VALENTINE. I like the cucumber.

WAITER. Right, sir. (Summing up.) Claret cup, syphon, one Scotch and one Irish?

MRS. CLANDON. I think that's right.

WAITER (perfectly happy). Right, ma'am. Directly, ma'am. Thank you. (He ambles off through the window, having sounded the whole gamut of human happiness, from the bottom to the top, in a little over two minutes.)

McCOMAS. We can begin now, I suppose?

BOHUN. We had better wait until Mrs. Clandon's husband arrives.

CRAMPTON. What d'y' mean? I'm her husband.

BOHUN (instantly pouncing on the inconsistency between this and his previous statement). You said just now your name was Crampton.

CRAMPTON. So it is.

MRS. CLANDON	} (all four	{ I---
GLORIA	} speaking	{ My---
McCOMAS	} simul-	{ Mrs.---
VALENTINE	} taneously).	{ You---

BOHUN (drowning them in two thunderous words). One moment. (Dead silence.) Pray allow me. Sit down everybody. (They obey humbly. Gloria takes the saddle-bag chair on the hearth. Valentine slips around to her side of the room and sits on the ottoman facing the window, so that he can look at her. Crampton sits on the ottoman with

93

his back to Valentine's. Mrs. Clandon, who has all along kept at the opposite side of the room in order to avoid Crampton as much as possible, sits near the door, with McComas beside her on her left. Bohun places himself magisterially in the centre of the group, near the corner of the table on Mrs. Clandon's side. When they are settled, he fixes Crampton with his eye, and begins.) In this family, it appears, the husband's name is Crampton: the wife's Clandon. Thus we have on the very threshold of the case an element of confusion.

VALENTINE (getting up and speaking across to him with one knee on the ottoman). But it's perfectly simple.

BOHUN (annihilating him with a vocal thunderbolt). It is. Mrs. Clandon has adopted another name. That is the obvious explanation which you feared I could not find out for myself. You mistrust my intelligence, Mr. Valentine--- (Stopping him as he is about to protest.) No: I don't want you to answer that: I want you to think over it when you feel your next impulse to interrupt me.

VALENTINE (dazed). This is simply breaking a butterfly on a wheel. What does it matter? (He sits down again.)

BOHUN. I will tell you what it matters, sir. It matters that if this family difference is to be smoothed over as we all hope it may be, Mrs. Clandon, as a matter of social convenience and decency, will have to resume her husband's name. (Mrs. Clandon assumes an expression of the most determined obstinacy.) Or else Mr. Crampton will have to call himself Mr. Clandon. (Crampton looks indomitably resolved to do nothing of the sort.) No doubt you think that an easy matter, Mr. Valentine. (He looks pointedly at Mrs. Clandon, then at Crampton.) I differ from you. (He throws himself back in his chair, frowning heavily.)

McCOMAS (timidly). I think, Bohun, we had perhaps better dispose of the important questions first.

BOHUN. McComas: there will be no difficulty about the important questions. There never is. It is the trifles that will wreck you at the harbor mouth. (McComas looks as if he considered this a paradox.) You don't agree with me, eh?

McCOMAS (flatteringly). If I did---

BOHUN (interrupting him). If you did, you would be me, instead of being what you are.

McCOMAS (fawning on him). Of course, Bohun, your specialty---

BOHUN (again interrupting him). My specialty is being right when other people are wrong. If you agreed with me I should be of no use here. (He nods at him to drive the point home; then turns suddenly and forcibly on Crampton.) Now you, Mr. Crampton: what point in this business have you most at heart?

CRAMPTON (beginning slowly). I wish to put all considerations of self aside in this matter---

BOHUN (interrupting him). So do we all, Mr. Crampton. (To Mrs. Clandon.) Y o u wish to put self aside, Mrs. Clandon?

MRS. CLANDON. Yes: I am not consulting my own feelings in being here.

BOHUN. So do you, Miss Clandon?

GLORIA. Yes.

BOHUN. I thought so. We all do.

VALENTINE. Except me. My aims are selfish.

BOHUN. That's because you think an impression of sincerity will produce a better effect on Miss Clandon than an impression of disinterestedness. (Valentine, utterly dismantled and destroyed by this just remark, takes refuge in a feeble, speechless smile. Bohun, satisfied at having now effectually crushed all rebellion, throws himself back in his chair, with an air of being prepared to listen tolerantly to their grievances.) Now, Mr. Crampton, go on. It's understood that self is put aside. Human nature always begins by saying that.

CRAMPTON. But I mean it, sir.

BOHUN. Quite so. Now for your point.

CRAMPTON. Every reasonable person will admit that it's an unselfish one---the children.

BOHUN. Well? What about the children?

CRAMPTON (with emotion). They have---

BOHUN (pouncing forward again). Stop. You're going to tell me about your feelings, Mr. Crampton. Don't: I sympathize with them; but they're not my business. Tell us exactly what you want: that's what we have to get at.

CRAMPTON (uneasily). It's a very difficult question to answer, Mr. Bohun.

BOHUN. Come: I'll help you out. What do you object to in the present circumstances of the children?

95

CRAMPTON. I object to the way they have been brought up.

BOHUN. How do you propose to alter that now?

CRAMPTON. I think they ought to dress more quietly.   *bader*

VALENTINE. Nonsense.

BOHUN (instantly flinging himself back in his chair, outraged by the interruption). When you are done, Mr. Valentine---when you are quite done.

VALENTINE. What's wrong with Miss Clandon's dress?

CRAMPTON (hotly to Valentine). My opinion is as good as yours.

GLORIA (warningly). Father!

CRAMPTON (subsiding piteously). I didn't mean you, my dear. (Pleading earnestly to Bohun.) But the two younger ones! you have not seen them, Mr. Bohun; and indeed I think you would agree with me that there is something very noticeable, something almost gay and frivolous in their style of dressing.

MRS. CLANDON (impatiently). Do you suppose I choose their clothes for them? Really this is childish.

CRAMPTON (furious, rising). Childish! (Mrs. Clandon rises indignantly.)

McCOMAS　} (all rising　} Crampton, you promised---

VALENTINE　} and speaking } Ridiculous. They dress charmingly.

GLORIA　} together).　} Pray let us behave reasonably.

Tumult. Suddenly they hear a chime of glasses in the room behind them. They turn in silent surprise and find that the waiter has just come back from the bar in the garden, and is jingling his tray warningly as he comes softly to the table with it.

WAITER (to Crampton, setting a tumbler apart on the table). Irish for you, sir. (Crampton sits down a little shamefacedly. The waiter sets another tumbler and a syphon apart, saying to Bohun) Scotch and syphon for you, sir. (Bohun waves his hand impatiently. The waiter places a large glass jug in the middle.) And claret cup. (All subside into their seats. Peace reigns.)

96

MRS. CLANDON (humbly to Bohun). I am afraid we interrupted you, Mr. Bohun.

BOHUN (calmly). You did. (To the waiter, who is going out.) Just wait a bit.

WAITER. Yes, sir. Certainly, sir. (He takes his stand behind Bohun's chair.)

MRS. CLANDON (to the waiter). You don't mind our detaining you, I hope. Mr. Bohun wishes it.

WAITER (now quite at his ease). Oh, no, ma'am, not at all, ma'am. It is a pleasure to me to watch the working of his trained and powerful mind---very stimulating, very entertaining and instructive indeed, ma'am.

BOHUN (resuming command of the proceedings). Now, Mr. Crampton: we are waiting for you. Do you give up your objection to the dressing, or do you stick to it?

CRAMPTON (pleading). Mr. Bohun: consider my position for a moment. I haven't got myself alone to consider: there's my sister Sophronia and my brother-in-law and all their circle. They have a great horror of anything that is at all---at all---well---

BOHUN. Out with it. Fast? Loud? Gay?

CRAMPTON. Not in any unprincipled sense of course; but---but--- (blurting it out desperately) those two children would shock them. They're not fit to mix with their own people. That's what I complain of.

MRS. CLANDON (with suppressed impatience). Mr. Valentine: do you think there is anything fast or loud about Phil and Dolly?

VALENTINE. Certainly not. It's utter bosh. Nothing can be in better taste.

CRAMPTON. Oh, yes: of course you say so.

MRS. CLANDON. William: you see a great deal of good English society. Are my children overdressed?

WAITER (reassuringly). Oh, dear, no, ma'am. (Persuasively.) Oh, no, sir, not at all. A little pretty and tasty no doubt; but very choice and classy---very genteel and high toned indeed. Might be the son and daughter of a Dean, sir, I assure you, sir. You have only to look at them, sir, to--- (At this moment a harlequin and columbine, dancing to the music of the band in the garden, which has just reached the coda of a waltz, whirl one another into the room. The harlequin's dress is made of lozenges, an inch square, of turquoise blue silk and gold alternately. His hat is gilt and his mask turned up. The columbine's petticoats are the epitome of a harvest field, golden orange and poppy crimson, with a tiny velvet jacket for the poppy stamens. They pass, an exquisite and dazzling apparition, between McComas and Bohun, and then back in a circle to the end of the table, where, as the final chord of the waltz is struck, they make a tableau in the middle of the company, the harlequin down on his left knee, and the columbine standing on his right knee, with her arms curved over her head. Unlike their dancing, which is charmingly graceful, their attitudinizing is hardly a success, and threatens to end in a catastrophe.)

THE COLUMBINE (screaming). Lift me down, somebody: I'm going to fall. Papa: lift me down.

CRAMPTON (anxiously running to her and taking her hands). My child!

DOLLY (jumping down with his help). Thanks: so nice of you. (Phil, putting his hat into his belt, sits on the side of the table and pours out some claret cup. Crampton returns to his place on the ottoman in great perplexity.) Oh, what fun! Oh, dear. (She seats herself with a vault on the front edge of the table, panting.) Oh, claret cup! (She drinks.)

BOHUN (in powerful tones). This is the younger lady, is it?

DOLLY (slipping down off the table in alarm at his formidable voice and manner). Yes, sir. Please, who are you?

MRS. CLANDON. This is Mr. Bohun, Dolly, who has very kindly come to help us this evening.

DOLLY. Oh, then he comes as a boon and a blessing---

PHILIP. Sh!

CRAMPTON. Mr. Bohun---McComas: I appeal to you. Is this right? Would you blame my sister's family for objecting to this?

DOLLY (flushing ominously). Have you begun again?

CRAMPTON (propitiating her). No, no. It's perhaps natural at your age.

DOLLY (obstinately). Never mind my age. Is it pretty?

CRAMPTON. Yes, dear, yes. (He sits down in token of submission.)

DOLLY (following him insistently). Do you like it?

CRAMPTON. My child: how can you expect me to like it or to approve of it?

DOLLY (determined not to let him off). How can you think it pretty and not like it?

McCOMAS (rising, angry and scandalized). Really I must say--- (Bohun, who has listened to Dolly with the highest approval, is down on him instantly.)

BOHUN. No: don't interrupt, McComas. The young lady's method is right. (To Dolly, with tremendous emphasis.) Press your questions, Miss Clandon: press your questions.

DOLLY (rising). Oh, dear, you are a regular overwhelmer! Do you always go on like this?

BOHUN (rising). Yes. Don't you try to put me out of countenance, young lady: you're too young to do it. (He takes McComas's chair from beside Mrs. Clandon's and sets it beside his own.) Sit down. (Dolly, fascinated, obeys; and Bohun sits down again. McComas, robbed of his seat, takes a chair on the other side between the table and the ottoman.) Now, Mr. Crampton, the facts are before you---both of them. You think you'd like to have your two youngest children to live with you. Well, you wouldn't--- (Crampton tries to protest; but Bohun will not have it on any terms.) No, you wouldn't: you think you would; but I know better than you. You'd want this young lady here to give up dressing like a stage columbine in the evening and like a fashionable columbine in the morning. Well, she won't---never. She thinks she will; but---

DOLLY (interrupting him). No I don't. (Resolutely.) I'll n e v e r give up dressing prettily. Never. As Gloria said to that man in Madeira, never, never, never while grass grows or water runs. *reaction*

VALENTINE (rising in the wildest agitation). What! What! (Beginning to speak very fast.) When did she say that? Who did she say that to?

BOHUN (throwing himself back with massive, pitying remonstrance). Mr. Valentine---

VALENTINE (pepperily). Don't you interrupt me, sir: this is something really serious. I i n s i s t on knowing who Miss Clandon said that to.

DOLLY. Perhaps Phil remembers. Which was it, Phil? number three or number five?

VALENTINE. Number five!!!

PHILIP. Courage, Valentine. It wasn't number five: it was only a tame naval lieutenant that was always on hand---the most patient and harmless of mortals. _cut_ _Valentine_

GLORIA (coldly). What are we discussing now, pray?

VALENTINE (very red). Excuse me: I am sorry I interrupted. I shall intrude no further, Mrs. Clandon. (He bows to Mrs. Clandon and marches away into the garden, boiling with suppressed rage.)

DOLLY. Hmhm!

PHILIP. Ahah!

GLORIA. Please go on, Mr. Bohun.

DOLLY (striking in as Bohun, frowning formidably, collects himself for a fresh grapple with the case). You're going to bully us, Mr. Bohun.

BOHUN. I---

DOLLY (interrupting him). Oh, yes, you are: you think you're not; but you are. I know by your eyebrows.

BOHUN (capitulating). Mrs. Clandon: these are clever children--- clear headed, well brought up children. I make that admission deliberately. Can you, in return, point out to me any way of inducting them to hold their tongues?

MRS. CLANDON. Dolly, dearest---!

PHILIP. Our old failing, Dolly. Silence! (Dolly holds her mouth.)

MRS. CLANDON. Now, Mr. Bohun, before they begin again---

WAITER (softer). Be quick, sir: be quick.

DOLLY (beaming at him). Dear ~~William~~! _Boss_ → _emphatic_

PHILIP. Sh!

BOHUN (unexpectedly beginning by hurling a question straight at Dolly). Have you any intention of getting married?

DOLLY. I! Well, Finch calls me by my Christian name.

McCOMAS. I will not have this. Mr. Bohun: I use the young lady's Christian name naturally as an old friend of her mother's.

DOLLY. Yes, you call me Dolly as an old friend of my mother's. But what about Dorothee-ee-a? (McComas rises indignantly.)

CRAMPTON (anxiously, rising to restrain him). Keep your temper, McComas. Don't let us quarrel. Be patient.

McCOMAS. I will not be patient. You are shewing the most wretched weakness of character, Crampton. I say this is monstrous.

DOLLY. Mr. Bohun: please bully Finch for us.

BOHUN. I will. McComas: you're making yourself ridiculous. Sit down.

McCOMAS. I---

BOHUN (waving him down imperiously). No: sit down, sit down. (McComas sits down sulkily; and Crampton, much relieved, follows his example.)

DOLLY (to Bohun, meekly). Thank you.

BOHUN. Now, listen to me, all of you. I give no opinion, McComas, as to how far you may or may not have committed yourself in the direction indicated by this young lady. (McComas is about to protest.) No: don't interrupt me: if she doesn't marry you she will marry somebody else. That is the solution of the difficulty as to her not bearing her father's name. The other lady intends to get married.

GLORIA (flushing). Mr. Bohun!

BOHUN. Oh, yes, you do: you don't know it; but you do.

GLORIA (rising). Stop. I warn you, Mr. Bohun, not to answer for my intentions.

BOHUN (rising). It's no use, Miss Clandon: you can't put me down. I tell you your name will soon be neither Clandon nor Crampton; and I could tell you what it will be if I chose. (He goes to the other end of the table, where he unrolls his domino, and puts the false nose on the table. When he moves they all rise; and Phil goes to the window. Bohun, with a gesture, summons the waiter to help him in robing.) Mr. Crampton: your notion of going to law is all nonsense: your children will be of age before you could get the point decided. (Allowing the waiter to put the domino on his shoulders.) You can do nothing but make a friendly arrangement. If you want your family more than they want you, you'll get the worse of the arrangement: if they want you more than you want them, you'll get the better of it. (He shakes the domino into becoming folds and takes up the false nose. Dolly gazes admiringly at him.) The strength of their position lies in their being very agreeable people personally. The strength of your position lies in your income. (He claps on the false nose, and is again grotesquely transfigured.)

DOLLY (running to him). Oh, now you look quite like a human being. Mayn't I have just one dance with you? C a n you dance? (Phil, resuming his part of harlequin, waves his hat as if casting a spell on them.)

BOHUN (thunderously). Yes: you think I can't; but I can. Come along. (He seizes her and dances off with her through the window in a most powerful manner, but with studied propriety and grace. The waiter is meanwhile busy putting the chairs back in their customary places.)

PHILIP. "On with the dance: let joy be unconfined." William! *Bess*

WAITER. Yes, sir.

PHILIP. Can you procure a couple of dominos and false noses for my father and Mr. McComas?

McCOMAS. Most certainly not. I protest---

CRAMPTON. No, no. What harm will it do, just for once, McComas? Don't let us be spoil-sports.

McCOMAS. Crampton: you are not the man I took you for. (Pointedly.) Bullies are always cowards. (He goes disgustedly towards the window.)

CRAMPTON (following him). Well, never mind. We must indulge them a little. Can you get us something to wear, waiter? *ness*

WAITER. Certainly, sir. (He precedes them to the window, and stands aside there to let them pass out before him.) This way, sir. Dominos and noses, sir?

McCOMAS (angrily, on his way out). I shall wear my own nose.

WAITER (suavely). Oh, dear, yes, sir: the false one will fit over it quite easily, sir: plenty of room, sir, plenty of room. (He goes out after McComas.)

CRAMPTON (turning at the window to Phil with an attempt at genial fatherliness). Come along, my boy, come along. (He goes.)

PHILIP (cheerily, following him). Coming, dad, coming. (On the window threshold, he stops; looking after Crampton; then turns fantastically with his bat bent into a halo round his head, and says with

102

a lowered voice to Mrs. Clandon and Gloria) Did you feel the pathos of that? (He vanishes.)

MRS. CLANDON (left alone with Gloria). Why did Mr. Valentine go away so suddenly, I wonder?

GLORIA (petulantly). I don't know. Yes, I d o know. Let us go and see the dancing. (They go towards the window, and are met by Valentine, who comes in from the garden walking quickly, with his face set and sulky.)

VALENTINE (stiffly). Excuse me. I thought the party had quite broken up.

GLORIA (nagging). Then why did you come back?

VALENTINE. I came back because I am penniless. I can't get out that way without a five shilling ticket.

MRS. CLANDON. Has anything annoyed you, Mr. Valentine?

GLORIA. Never mind him, mother. This is a fresh insult to me: that is all.

MRS. CLANDON (hardly able to realize that Gloria is deliberately provoking an altercation). Gloria!

VALENTINE. Mrs. Clandon: have I said anything insulting? Have I done anything insulting?

GLORIA. you have implied that my past has been like yours. That is the worst of insults.

VALENTINE. I imply nothing of the sort. I declare that my past has been blameless in comparison with yours.

MRS. CLANDON (most indignantly). Mr. Valentine!

VALENTINE. Well, what am I to think when I learn that Miss Clandon has made exactly the same speeches to other men that she has made to me---when I hear of at least five former lovers, with a tame naval lieutenant thrown in? Oh, it's too bad.

MRS. CLANDON. But you surely do not believe that these affairs--- mere jokes of the children's---were serious, Mr. Valentine?

VALENTINE. Not to you---not to her, perhaps. But I know what the men felt. (With ludicrously genuine earnestness.) Have you ever thought of the wrecked lives, the marriages contracted in the recklessness of despair, the suicides, the---the---the---

103

GLORIA (interrupting him contemptuously). Mother: this man is a sentimental idiot. (She sweeps away to the fireplace.)

MRS. CLANDON (shocked). Oh, my d e a r e s t Gloria, Mr. Valentine will think that rude.

VALENTINE. I am not a sentimental idiot. I am cured of sentiment for ever. (He sits down in dudgeon.)

MRS. CLANDON. Mr. Valentine: you must excuse us all. Women have to unlearn the false good manners of their slavery before they acquire the genuine good manners of their freedom. Don't think Gloria vulgar (Gloria turns, astonished): she is not really so.

GLORIA. Mother! You apologize for me to h i m!

MRS. CLANDON. My dear: you have some of the faults of youth as well as its qualities; and Mr. Valentine seems rather too old fashioned in his ideas about his own sex to like being called an idiot. And now had we not better go and see what Dolly is doing? (She goes towards the window. Valentine rises.)

GLORIA. Do you go, mother. I wish to speak to Mr. Valentine alone.

MRS. CLANDON (startled into a remonstrance). My dear! (Recollecting herself.) I beg your pardon, Gloria. Certainly, if you wish. (She bows to Valentine and goes out.)

VALENTINE. Oh, if your mother were only a widow! She's worth six of you.

GLORIA. That is the first thing I have heard you say that does you honor.

VALENTINE. Stuff! Come: say what you want to say and let me go.

GLORIA. I have only this to say. You dragged me down to your level for a moment this afternoon. Do you think, if that had ever happened before, that I should not have been on my guard---that I should not have known what was coming, and known my own miserable weakness?

VALENTINE (scolding at her passionately). Don't talk of it in that way. What do I care for anything in you but your weakness, as you call it? You thought yourself very safe, didn't you, behind your advanced ideas! I amused myself by upsetting t h e m pretty easily.

GLORIA (insolently, feeling that now she can do as she likes with him). Indeed!

VALENTINE. But why did I do it? Because I was being tempted to awaken your heart---to stir the depths in you. Why was I tempted? Because Nature was in deadly earnest with me when I was in jest with her. When the great moment came, who was awakened? who was stirred? in whom did the depths break up? In myself--- m y s e l f: I was transported: you were only offended---shocked. You were only an ordinary young lady, too ordinary to allow tame lieutenants to go as far as I went. That's all. I shall not trouble you with conventional apologies. Good-bye. (He makes resolutely for the door.)

GLORIA. Stop. (He hesitates.) Oh, will you understand, if I tell you the truth, that I am not making an advance to you?

VALENTINE. Pooh! I know what you're going to say. You think you're not ordinary---that I was right---that you really have those depths in your nature. It flatters you to believe it. (She recoils.) Well, I grant that you are not ordinary in some ways: you are a clever girl (Gloria stifles an exclamation of rage, and takes a threatening step towards him); but you've not been awakened yet. You didn't care: you don't care. It was my tragedy, not yours. Good-bye. (He turns to the door. She watches him, appalled to see him slipping from her grasp. As he turns the handle, he pauses; then turns again to her, offering his hand.) Let us part kindly.

GLORIA (enormously relieved, and immediately turning her back on him deliberately.) Good-bye. I trust you will soon recover from the wound.

VALENTINE (brightening up as it flashes on him that he is master of the situation after all). I shall recover: such wounds heal more than they harm. After all, I still have my own Gloria.

GLORIA (facing him quickly). What do you mean?

VALENTINE. The Gloria of my imagination.

GLORIA (proudly). Keep your own Gloria---the Gloria of your imagination. (Her emotion begins to break through her pride.) The real Gloria---the Gloria who was shocked, offended, horrified---oh, yes, quite truly---who was driven almost mad with shame by the feeling that all her power over herself had been broken down at her first real encounter with---with--- (The color rushes over her face again. She covers it with her left hand, and puts her right on his left arm to support herself.)

VALENTINE. Take care. I'm losing my senses again. (Summoning all her courage, she takes away her hand from her face and puts it on his right shoulder, turning him towards her and looking him straight in the eyes. He begins to protest agitatedly.) Gloria: be sensible: it's no use: I haven't a penny in the world.

GLORIA. Can't you earn one? Other people do.

VALENTINE (half delighted, half frightened). I never could---you'd be unhappy--- My dearest love: I should be the merest fortune-hunting adventurer if--- (Her grip on his arms tightens; and she kisses him.) Oh, Lord! (Breathless.) Oh, I--- (He gasps.) I don't know anything about women: twelve years' experience is not enough. (In a gust of jealousy she throws him away from her; and he reels her back into the chair like a leaf before the wind, as Dolly dances in, waltzing with the waiter, followed by Mrs. Clandon and Finch, also waltzing, and Phil pirouetting by himself.)

DOLLY (sinking on the chair at the writing-table). Oh, I'm out of breath. How beautifully you waltz, William!

MRS. CLANDON (sinking on the saddlebag seat on the hearth). Oh, how could you make me do such a silly thing, Finch! I haven't danced since the soiree at South Place twenty years ago.

GLORIA (peremptorily at Valentine). Get up. (Valentine gets up abjectly.) Now let us have no false delicacy. Tell my mother that we have agreed to marry one another. (A silence of stupefaction ensues. Valentine, dumb with panic, looks at them with an obvious impulse to run away.)

DOLLY (breaking the silence). Number Six!

PHILIP. Sh!

DOLLY (tumultuously). Oh, my feelings! I want to kiss somebody; and we bar it in the family. Where's Finch?

McCOMAS (starting violently). No, positively--- (Crampton appears in the window.)

DOLLY (running to Crampton). Oh, you're just in time. (She kisses him.) Now (leading him forward) bless them.

GLORIA. No. I will have no such thing, even in jest. When I need a blessing, I shall ask my mother's.

CRAMPTON (to Gloria, with deep disappointment). Am I to understand that you have engaged yourself to this young gentleman?

GLORIA (resolutely). Yes. Do you intend to be our friend or---

DOLLY (interposing). ---or our father?

CRAMPTON. I should like to be both, my child. But surely---! Mr. Valentine: I appeal to your sense of honor.

106

VALENTINE. You're quite right. It's perfect madness. If we go out to dance together I shall have to borrow five shillings from her for a ticket. Gloria: don't be rash: you're throwing yourself away. I'd much better clear straight out of this, and never see any of you again. I shan't commit suicide: I shan't even be unhappy. It'll be a relief to me: I---I'm frightened, I'm positively frightened; and that's the plain truth.

GLORIA (determinedly). You shall not go.

VALENTINE (quailing). No, dearest: of course not. But--oh, will somebody only talk sense for a moment and bring us all to reason! I can't. Where's Bohun? Bohun's the man. Phil: go and summon Bohun---

PHILIP. From the vastly deep. I go. (He makes his bat quiver in the air and darts away through the window.)

WAITER (harmoniously to Valentine). If you will excuse my putting in a word, sir, do not let a matter of five shillings stand between you and your happiness, sir. We shall be only too pleased to put the ticket down to you: and you can settle at your convenience. Very glad to meet you in any way, very happy and pleased indeed, sir.

PHILIP (re-appearing). He comes. (He waves his bat over the window. Bohun comes in, taking off his false nose and throwing it on the table in passing as he comes between Gloria and Valentine.)

VALENTINE. The point is, Mr. Bohun---

McCOMAS (interrupting from the hearthrug). Excuse me, sir: the point must be put to him by a solicitor. The question is one of an engagement between these two young people. The lady has some property, and (looking at Crampton) will probably have a good deal more.

CRAMPTON. Possibly. I hope so.

VALENTINE. And the gentleman hasn't a rap.

BOHUN (nailing Valentine to the point instantly). Then insist on a settlement. That shocks your delicacy: most sensible precautions do. But you ask my advice; and I give it to you. Have a settlement.

GLORIA (proudly). He shall have a settlement.

VALENTINE. My good sir, I don't want advice for myself. Give h e r some advice.

BOHUN. She won't take it. When you're married, she won't take yours either--- (turning suddenly on Gloria) oh, no, you won't: you think you will; but you won't. He'll set to work and earn his living--- (turning suddenly to Valentine) oh, yes, you will: you think you won't; but you will. She'll make you.

CRAMPTON (only half persuaded). Then, Mr. Bohun, you don't think this match an unwise one?

BOHUN. Yes, I do: all matches are unwise. It's unwise to be born; it's unwise to be married; it's unwise to live; and it's unwise to die.

WAITER (insinuating himself between Crampton and Valentine). Then, if I may respectfully put in a word in, sir, so much the worse for wisdom! (To Valentine, benignly.) Cheer up, sir, cheer up: every man is frightened of marriage when it comes to the point; but it often turns out very comfortable, very enjoyable and happy indeed, sir---from time to time. I never was master in my own house, sir: my wife was like your young lady: she was of a commanding and masterful disposition, which my son has inherited. But if I had my life to live twice over, I'd do it again, I'd do it again, I assure you. You never can tell, sir: you never can tell.

PHILIP. Allow me to remark that if Gloria has made up her mind---

DOLLY. The matter's settled and Valentine's done for. And we're missing all the dances.

VALENTINE (to Gloria, gallantly making the best of it). May I have a dance---

BOHUN (interposing in his grandest diapason). Excuse me: I claim that privilege as counsel's fee. May I have the honor---thank you. (He dances away with Gloria and disappears among the lanterns, leaving Valentine gasping.)

VALENTINE (recovering his breath). Dolly: may I--- (offering himself as her partner)?

DOLLY. Nonsense! (Eluding him and running round the table to the fireplace.) Finch---my Finch! (She pounces on McComas and makes him dance.)

McCOMAS (protesting). Pray restrain --- really --- (He is borne off dancing through the window.)

VALENTINE (making a last effort). Mrs. Clandon: may I---

PHILIP (forestalling him). Come, mother. (He seizes his mother and whirls her away.)

MRS. CLANDON (remonstrating).   Phil, Phil--- (She shares McComas's fate.)

CRAMPTON (following them with senile glee). Ho! ho! He! he! he! (He goes into the garden chuckling at the fun.)

VALENTINE (collapsing on the ottoman and staring at the waiter). I might as well be a married man already. (The waiter contemplates the captured Duellist of Sex with affectionate commiseration, shaking his head slowly.)

CURTAIN.

Lightning Source UK Ltd.
Milton Keynes UK
23 January 2010
149027UK00001B/301/P